CATS IN THE CRATER

MY FANGTASTICALLY EVIL VAMPIRE PET

CATS IN THE CRATER

MO O'HARA
ILLUSTRATED BY MAREK JAGUCKI

FEIWEL AND FRIENDS ❖ NEW YORK

A Feiwel and Friends Book
An imprint of Macmillan Publishing Group, LLC
120 Broadway, New York, NY 10271

Our books may be purchased in bulk for promotional, educational, or business use. Please contact your local bookseller or the Macmillan Corporate and Premium Sales Department at (800) 221-7945 ext. 5442 or by email at MacmillanSpecialMarkets@ macmillan.com.

Library of Congress Control Number: 2019940844

ISBN 978-1-250-12815-7 (hardcover) / ISBN 978-1-250-12816-4 (ebook)

Book design by Sophie Erb

Feiwel and Friends logo designed by Filomena Tuosto

First edition, 2020

10 9 8 7 6 5 4 3 2 1

mackids.com

To all my writer and illustrator friends, who
challenge me and inspire me to write, and
to my cats, who distract me and would
rather I just play with them
—M.O.

For Mila
—M.J.

CATS IN THE CRATER

To be honest, so far, this Evil Scientist Summer camp has had lots of ups and downs. (Mostly, up in rockets and down in snake pits.) But my main goal hasn't changed. So maybe this week will have lots of ups (winning challenges, having the camp counselors tell me how totally epic I am, actually beating Igor in arm wrestling) or maybe it will have downs (no more snakes, though, OK?), but I know one thing: at the end of next week I am wearing the Evil Emperor of the Week crown.

I have an evil fridge magnet that I brought with me to camp. (Well, it was an ordinary fridge magnet. I just added the word "evil" in marker.) Evil plans + evil energy + evil determination = evil success.

I've got the plans, the energy and the determination so I can equal the evil success! This is my week to do it. So bring it on camp Mwhaaa-haa-ha-a-watha. You are looking at your new Evil Emperor.

Mwhaaa-haa-haaa-ha-ha,

The Great and Powerful Mark

1

"Rrreeeeoooowwww!"

"Fang, you have to get under the bed," I pleaded. "I know it's a bit smelly." I flicked away some old gym socks that had been under there since the beginning of the summer, probably. "Yuck. Yeah, OK, pretty smelly, but you have to get under there anyway. They called an immediate tent search for pets! And you know what happens if they find you. It'll be the Canoe of Shame for both of us."

"Urgh, urgh, urgh, urgh," said my Evil Scientist tentmate Igor, who is a kid of few words. OK, one word.

I translated the urghs. "Yeah, or they'll put us in the 'I-Stupidly-Tried-to-Break-the-Rules-and-Smuggle-in-a-Pet' Stockade and call Mom to come and get us!"

"Urgh, urgh, urgh," Igor added, looking out from the front flap of the tent.

"They are almost here, Fang. You've got to hide," I said, trying to shove her. She's tiny, but when she wants to she can spread herself out so wide that you can't bend her, let alone hide her somewhere that she doesn't want to be hid.

"She's not budging," I said, and let go of Fang. She relaxed her claws, leaped up onto the bed with a smug "Meow" and started to wash herself.

"Fang, you are gonna get us kicked out of camp," I said.

"Urgh, urgh, urgh!" Igor rushed over toward us as I heard footsteps approaching the tent flap.

Igor must have caught Fang off guard because

she didn't claw him when he scooped her up. I don't know what he was thinking, but in a split second, just as the tent flap opened, Igor threw Fang up into the air. We were both pretty surprised when she didn't come down again.

Phillipe Fortescue, master of evil disguise, and Kirsty Katastrophe, evil cheerleader at large, strode into the tent and looked around.

"You know why we are here," Phillipe said. "There has been a pet found in one of the tents."

"Urgh, urgh, urgh?" Igor nodded, trying desperately not to look up to see where the heck Fang had gone.

"Well, no pets here," I said, putting my hand on each of their shoulders and guiding Kirsty and Phillipe toward the tent flap. "Thanks for checking, though."

Kirsty judo-flipped me onto the floor. "Owwwh," I mumbled.

"We are not done looking," she said, and walked over to where I had been standing before. The first place she checked was under my bed. "No animal could live under there. It stinks," she said. Then she looked under the blankets and around the bottom of the bed.

As I sat up, rubbing my head from where it had thwacked the floor, I spotted Fang.

She was hanging upside down from the tent roof like a little bat kitty. And she didn't look happy to be there. I jerked my head back toward Kirsty quickly so she wouldn't see me looking up.

Igor hadn't spotted Fang yet.

"So what pet did you find?" I asked, getting up and speaking to Phillipe.

"It was a turtle. Apparently, it had been in hibernation and the camper had disguised it as a rock. It wasn't until it tried to crawl out of the tent and got stuck upside down in the dirt that someone noticed that the rock could move."

"Urgh, urgh," Igor said, shaking his head.

"Yeah, poor kid," I echoed.

Kirsty upended my mattress and shook it while she spoke. "If you're hiding something, then it'll be easier to tell us now."

I snatched a glance and saw that one of Fang's claws had slipped off from the tent canvas. She was tilting now and hanging like a bat kitty with a wonky claw.

"Soooo, do you go easy on a kid if they confess to having a pet, then?" I said.

"No." She laughed. "I meant it would be easier *for us*. We have a lot to do before our special guest gets here, and I don't want to keep looking for any more contraband pets." She dropped the mattress and it fell to the floor. "Come on, Phillipe, let's go."

As the tent flap closed behind them, I pointed to the ceiling.

"Urgh," Igor said as he looked up just in time to see Fang unhook her final claw and tumble onto the mattress.

The tent flap burst open again.

"Arrrgh!" I jumped toward the mattress to cover Fang. "How did that wild cougar kitten get into our tent from the woods . . . ?" I started to say.

"Relax, it's just me," Geeky Girl, the only non-evil kid at Evil Scientist Summer Camp, said. "I wanted to see if you passed tent inspection."

"Yeah, just," I said. "And we learned that Fang is part bat." I laughed.

Igor did a pretty good impression of an

upside-down bat Fang and giggled too. I don't think I had ever heard Igor giggle. It's kinda like a very low gurgly growl with shoulder shaking.

"Anyway, yeah, we passed. I guess Boris was out on a tree branch somewhere?" I added. "How does nobody notice a bright green budgie flying around camp?"

"People don't look up very much, I guess." She reached down and stroked Fang. "Plus, he's pretty good at sensing danger," Geeky Girl said. "Speaking of danger, everyone is on edge about this new special visitor. Something doesn't feel right. You guys might want to stash Fang somewhere safe and come outside."

2

We put on our white coats and Fang jumped into my pocket as we followed Geeky Girl out of the tent. Everyone was milling around in the clearing between the tents. There was a buzz about who would be visiting the camp. Plus, people were pointing to the kid with the pet turtle who was being taken to the stockade until his parents could come and get him. He stared at the ground, solemnly carrying his turtle with the words *Evil Rocks* painted on its shell. Fang squirmed in my pocket.

"That can't be us, Fang," I whispered. "I've got way too much I still want to do at Camp Mwhaaa-haa-ha-a-watha."

Rumors about this week's celebrity villain

filled the air. Some said it was probably Mangus the Mean, a cool Viking villain who just won *Celebrity Villain Bake-Off.* As well as rampaging and generally cool, retro Viking villainy, he could also make really awesome evil pineapple upside-down cake.

Some said it was going to be Tim the Terrifying. He is this old-school evil villain who wears a mask and has these big claw gloves and stuff to make him look really, well, terrifying I guess. But it always just makes me think, when he takes off that stuff, he probably just looks like an accountant. And not even a particularly evil accountant, really.

"You know," I said to Geeky Girl and Igor, "I always thought that he should have changed his name. I mean, he earned his reputation and all, but you just have to try twice as hard with a name like Tim the Terrifying, don't you."

Dustin and Sanj came up to us and asked if we had heard anything.

"We heard that the campers are going to be taken somewhere tropical this week," Dustin said.

"That Goth Girl has ordered a whole case of sunblock just in case," Sanj said.

"What is her actual name, anyway? Goth Girl?" I said. "I mean, I've always been too scared to ask her, but someone must have."

"She threatened to shave my head once just because I looked at her. I'm not asking," Dustin said.

"It's probably much cooler and more evil sounding than *your* real name, Geeky Girl. What is it again? Glynis?" Sanj said, smirking.

Geeky Girl stepped forward to unsmirk Sanj's face when I interrupted, "Ha, ha. So not funny, Sanj. So, come on, who will the celebrity villain be?"

"Urgh, urgh, urgh, urgh," Igor added.

"What?" I said. "OK, this rumor stuff is getting out of hand if someone seriously thought that

Darth Vader was going to be our celebrity villain."

Igor looked slightly embarrassed.

"Oh, come on," Geeky Girl said, shaking her head.

You know what? I didn't care who it was; I just wanted to win Evil Emperor of the Week for myself and get a crown. It's not a lot for a guy to ask, really. In my head I was picturing the camp crowning ceremony where everyone had to kneel and chant, "Mark is an Epically Evil Emperor of the Week. All hail Emperor Mark," when Igor nudged me.

And when Igor nudges anyone it usually means they fall over.

I fell over.

"Hey, what was that for? I was having the best daydream—" I started to say, but then I felt it.

"Tornado!" Sanj squealed.

"Don't be ridiculous," Geeky Girl said. "There will be a reasonable scientific explanation for this."

"I've never been in a tornado, but I always thought the wind was kinda . . . you know . . . spinning more," I said. "This is more pushy wind than spinny."

"That's your scientific explanation?" Geeky Girl said.

But it was true. It was like there were waves of air blasting down onto the ground and causing the tents to shake and the ground to vibrate from the noise and pressure.

Then suddenly the sky got very dark.

"Remember how I said people never look up?" Geeky Girl gulped. "Look up now."

Something very, very large loomed in the air.

12

"Urgh, urgh, urgh!" Igor shouted.

"It's not the Death Star, Igor!" I shouted back as whatever it was got pretty loud.

It was massive, though, and it was floating right above the camp.

Fang went into complete instinct-predator-avoidance mode. She jumped out of my pocket and adopted Cat Attack stance between my legs. It's like centuries of avoiding things swooping out of the skies to get ground mammals gives them this fear of things overhead.  Luckily, every eye in the camp was looking up at whatever the heck that thing was.

It started to move toward the lake. As it did, I scooped up Fang and dropped her back into my pocket. "If we have to get away fast, kitten, then I need you ready to go," I whispered. But the thing started to drop down over the lake. I don't know what I expected to see as it came down, maybe laser beam cannons or robot warriors or something.

"It can't be," Dustin said.

"It looks like it," Sanj said.

As it descended, you could see that the flat rocky bit on the bottom was just that—rock. The rest of the thing had trees and grass and—OMG! It had an actual volcano in the middle of it! It was a flying volcano island! Literally, a flying volcano island! It was the coolest thing ever. I was watching a flying island land in our lake!

Bob and Diablo ran over to the lake edge near us to get a closer look.

"It's her! It's gotta be her," said Bob.

Trevor the Tech-in-ator, one of the other counselors, stepped forward and pushed us aside.

"It's her," he said.

The kids all started screaming and clapping like they were at some pop-star concert or something.

"Who is it?" I asked. "I mean, whoever it is, they have the coolest volcano island and all, but who is it?"

Trevor continued, "She vas an evil scientist before zey discovered most modern science. She vas an evil scientist ven nobody even had an evil lair."

"What did they do?" I asked.

"They just hung out in evil ordinary houses," Phillipe said.

The kids all mumbled in awe.

"It was a dark time," he added.

"You mean it's actually *her*?" I said. "No way."

"Yes vay," Trevor said.

"So, this person invented the first evil volcano lair? OK." Geeky Girl nodded. "But who is she?"

"Madame Mako," Trevor and I said at the same time.

"Urgh, urgh, urgh, urgh," Igor added.

"Yeah, I always liked the whole shark thing with the name too," I said.

"Mako? That's a Tahitian name. That's so funny," Geeky Girl started to say, "that's the same name as my—"

"Glenda!!!" A booming voice echoed out from the island across the lake. A small, stocky woman in a long, straight black dress stood on the shore. She had her gray-and-black hair pulled tightly back in a bun, pierced with a long jade dagger that looked way more lethal than a hair decoration.

I guess when you are an actual evil empress
you stick to accessories that double as weapons.
Weirdly, she was pointing toward the camp, and . . .
right at us.

"No?!" Geeky Girl started to back away. "It
can't be."

"Who's Glenda? Ooooh, I remember. That's
your—" I started to say but stopped talking when I
saw Geeky Girl's face.

"Come here, child," the old woman shouted,
and held out her arms. "Come and give your
grandmother a nice evil hug."

3

The sea of campers parted and everyone stood looking at Geeky Girl staring across the lake.

"She's your grandma?" I whispered.

"Yeah." Geeky Girl nodded.

"And you didn't know she was, like, the most famous evil scientist in like . . . evil science?" I asked.

"No," Geeky Girl answered. "Obviously not."

"I mean, you look up everything online. Didn't you ever look her up or anything?" I asked.

"No." She rolled her eyes. "Who Googles their grandma? Have you Googled your grandma?"

"My grandma lives in a condo upstate, and yours lives on a flying volcano island. More to Google there," I said.

"Don't dawdle, Glenda; I do detest dawdling," Madame Mako spoke again.

"You can't keep her waiting," Sanj said, and led Geeky Girl to the water's edge. I kept thinking she was gonna flatten Sanj any minute now for trying to take her arm, but she was just in a trance (and not an "I've been shot with a zombifying glare or ray gun or anything" kind of trance, just an "It's taking me a long, long time to process this stuff" kind of trance).

"Come on. Snap out of it," I mumbled.

"Let me help you, my dear, dear friend Glenda," he said as he led her over.

Finally, the complete weirdness of Sanj's words snapped her out of it.

"Get off." She shook her arm free. "I'm fine now and I'm not your dear, dear anything, got it?" she added.

Sanj stepped back.

Madame Mako pressed a button on a remote control that she carried, and a bridge shot out from her island to the edge of the lake where Geeky Girl stood. She looked across the bridge at her grandmother and then started to cross.

This was an awesome moment for Geeky Girl. So why did I feel on edge? Maybe it was Fang clawing and scratching in my pocket to get out? Her kitty danger sense was kicking in about something, but it might have just been that she was within ten feet of Sanj. That's enough to set her off. I held my pocket closed so she couldn't leap out. We were not going to be thrown out of camp in front of Madame Mako!

"It's OK, Fang. She's Geeky Girl's family. She'll be fine," I whispered. The words had just left my mouth when I spotted how completely not fine it was.

When Geeky Girl was maybe halfway across, a huge lizard, the size of a Rottweiler but with short legs, burst out of a door behind Madame Mako and came galloping toward Geeky Girl. She turned to run but her foot got caught in a slat on the bridge. Saliva dripped from the lizard's jaws as he moved. I ran for the bridge, but the lizard was closer to Geeky Girl than I was.

Suddenly Boris swooped down from a branch

and dive-bombed the lizard. It took one swipe of his powerful tail to thwack Boris out of the sky. He lay motionless on the bridge, well out of Geeky Girl's reach. The lizard didn't even slow down. He pelted toward her, thundering across the bridge. Madame Mako looked slightly irritated. Slightly irritated that this thing might eat her granddaughter!

Geeky Girl pulled at her foot while trying to kick the lizard hurtling toward her with her free leg. With no time to think about what I could actually do to stop a giant lizard, I jumped in front of it. The lizard made a low growling noise and a truly terrifying slurp as it got within reach. Just before its jaws snapped shut around my leg, Madame Mako whistled. The death lizard immediately slid to a halt.

"Heel, Lucky," she called, and the lizard trotted over to

her side, swishing its long tail as it went. I leaned over Geeky Girl and helped her yank her foot free. Then she crawled to Boris. His eyes rolled around a bit but then fixed on hers.

"You OK?" she asked him. He shook his head but then flap ped up to a low branch on a nearby palm tree.

We walked toward Madame Mako.

"Is that little bird your evil sidekick?" she said to Geeky Girl.

"That's Boris," she said.

"It is useful to have a pet sidekick sometimes to intimidate your enemies." She looked Boris up and down. "I'm not sure the budgie is the best choice for you, but we can work on this," she said. "And this is Lucky, my evil Komodo dragon."

Boris fluffed his feathers and totally taunted the dragon. Lucky snapped but Madame Mako tugged on his chain and he lay down by her feet. Fang was wriggling in my pocket, trying to get free. I couldn't risk anyone seeing her, though.

Madam Mako's lips tilted slightly up so that it looked like her face was trying to smile. "I am so glad I came to see you."

"You came to judge the contest at camp," Geeky Girl said.

"I came to see my promising evil grand-daughter," Madame Mako said.

She turned to me. "So who is this? Your henchman?"

"My henchman?" Geeky Girl laughed. "No way. This is Mark. He's at the camp too, but we also know each other from home." She looked at me. "Kinda," she added.

"Yeah, I'm an evil scientist too. I really admire your work, Madam Mako . . ." I held out my hand.

Madame Mako looked at me like she was considering feeding me to the death lizard and then thought that would be too messy. Instead, she said, "I wasn't talking *to* you, I was talking *about* you. Learn the difference."

"Ummm . . . yes . . . umm, I mean . . . will do" was all I could say as I let my hand drop to my side.

OK, I admit, I was totally burned by Madame Mako. I would expect nothing less. She was like evil royalty, and I had to earn her respect. But I was standing right near her and I had saved her granddaughter's life and, OK, she thought I was a henchman, but at least I was on her radar. By the end of this week, she was going to be crowning me Evil Emperor of the Week. I was just picturing her letting me drive the volcano island as part of the prize when she clapped her hands and brought me out of the dream. Then she turned again to Geeky Girl.

"Follow me. We better get started," Madame Mako said. She whistled again and Lucky padded along next to her on his gold chain. Geeky Girl and I followed her across the bridge to the camp.

All the counselors and campers bowed and curtsied as she passed. Some of them kept curtsying for Geeky Girl too. This was insane. Geeky Girl had joined the evil royal family!

Every single one of them stopped bowing as soon as I passed. Which was annoying, but fair enough, I guess. I wasn't royal yet, but I was determined to be emperor before the end of the week.

Madame Mako approached the front of the crowd. She held up her hand and silence fell.

"I am pleased to be here at . . ." She paused. Geeky Girl whispered in her ear, "at Camp Mwhaaa-haa-ha-a-watha." She did not look pleased, but I think she has a general resting "not that impressed with anything" face.

"Obviously, I invented the first evil lair. Your task for this week is to come up with an

innovative design for an evil lair, complete with ways of keeping it hidden and possible traps," she said.

"Um, no snake pits for the traps, OK?" I said, my skin still crawling from the first test of the summer.

"Urgh, urgh, urgh," Igor added.

"Oh yeah, and please no bears either, OK?" I translated.

"And no skunks or squirrels," Sanj said. "In fact, maybe we could agree on animal-free traps?"

"Silence." Madame Mako glared in our direction. "That is your task. Begin." She went back to her not-impressed face, and if it was possible, it looked even less impressed than before.

Kirsty stepped forward and welcomed Madame Mako to the camp and announced that there would be a luau in her honor that evening. The campers would all learn a traditional Tahitian dance and they would present her with their plans for their evil lairs.

I turned to Geeky Girl and whispered, "I can help you come up with an epically cool lair plan if you want to impress your grandma. We could work together on it. We make a pretty evil team, right?"

"I don't think I want to be on an evil team," Geeky Girl said.

I couldn't tell if she meant she didn't want to be on an *evil* team or that she didn't want to be on a *team* or if actually she'd decided she just really didn't want to be on a team with *me*, evil or otherwise. I was figuring it out when Madame Mako interrupted.

"Good," she said, turning to face us, "you don't need a team to succeed. You need to be strong and independent to lead an evil empire. That is not a team job. Who can quote for me from *Madame Mako's Evil Words of Wisdom* about this subject?" She turned to the campers.

Diablo spoke first. "Trust no one but yourself."

"Good," she said.

"When you stand at the top, you stand alone," Dustin said.

"Henchmen are helpful, but friends are a hindrance," Goth Girl shouted out.

"Very good." Madame Mako almost smiled. "What is your name?" she asked.

"Ezmirelda," Goth Girl answered. "With a Z. But people that actually know me call me Ez. There aren't many of those."

I heard Phillipe whisper to Trevor, "I never

actually knew her name and was a little afraid to ask."

I looked over at Igor and Geeky Girl. "That is way more evil than Glenda," I said.

"Way more evil than Mark," Geeky Girl answered.

"Urgh, urgh, urgh, urgh, urgh, urgh, urgh," Igor said.

"Umm, I think he said, 'Always be one step ahead of your opponent or have chess pieces that explode at will.' Is that right?" I said.

"Unfortunately . . . yes," Madame Mako said. "I had just invented some exploding chess pieces, and the publisher thought the quote would help the sales. I thought that one would be cut for the second edition. Never mind.

"The point is that you have to be strong in yourself to succeed. This task is to be completed on your own. No teams. No collaboration," she said, and turned to walk back to the island. "Granddaughter, I shall see you this evening. Work hard."

As she walked across the bridge, all the eyes in the camp turned to Geeky Girl.

People kept coming up to her. "OMG, you are soooo totally evil. I should have known," one girl said.

"You are so lucky to have a grandmother like that."

Trevor even came up to Geeky Girl, and said, "I could see the evil light in you ze whole time. I vas only so hard on you so you vould vork hard as your grandmother says."

"So now Geeky Girl is the evilest kid in camp?" I turned to Igor. "It's like an upside-down world."

"Urgh, urgh, urgh, urgh," he said.

"No, I don't think she looks like she's enjoying

it either. How could she not love all this evil attention?" I shook my head. "Let's get her out of here."

Igor nodded.

"She's too busy to talk to you now." I pushed past some people with pieces of paper, wanting autographs.

"Urgh, urgh, urgh, urgh," Igor echoed, and cleared a path for her to walk.

Kirsty stepped in front of us and blocked our way. She stared me down and I stepped aside so she could whisper something to Geeky Girl and hand her a piece of paper.

When we got back to Geeky Girl's tent, she flopped onto the bed.

"Urgh, urgh, urgh, urgh?" Igor asked.

"Kirsty gave me her résumé to pass on to Madame . . . Grandmother," she said. "Apparently her contract is up at the end of the summer and she wanted me to put in a good word for her about a job."

"Unbelievable," I said.

"I know," she said. "Kirsty Katastrophe is asking me to help her get a better evil job?"

"No, I mean, it's unbelievable. You are sooo lucky," I said. "She is the best grandma ever! You are related to the biggest evil celebrity on the planet!"

"I don't feel related to her," she said. "I don't know her, and she doesn't know me. And she didn't like Boris. I mean, who could not like Boris?"

As Boris flew through the tent flap and

fluttered down to Geeky Girl's shoulder, Fang
leaped out of my pocket and pounced. Boris was
too fast and flew out of reach again in a flutter
of feathers.

"I don't think she
would like Fang either,"
Geeky Girl said.

"Urgh, urgh, urgh, urgh," Igor added.

"Yeah, I agree. Boris just doesn't have the same strong evil vibe that Fang has," I said.

"What?" she said.

"Hey, Fang is fierce and intimidating and strikes fear into the heart of anyone who sees her," I said.

Then I looked over to see Fang rolling onto her back while Geeky Girl tickled her tummy with one of Boris's fallen feathers.

"She is truly terrifying." Geeky Girl smirked.

"Fang, you are letting the evil side down," I said, shaking my head. "So, what are you gonna do for your lair? Sanj and I came up with some great lair plans before camp."

"Urgh, urgh, urgh?" Igor asked.

"I think he'll either do the 'constantly moving untraceable by radar evil lair option A or B,'" I said.

"Urgh, urgh?" Igor asked.

"Option A is a prototype teleporting lair that is slightly out of phase with current space and time.

Option B is on the back of a giant evil elephant." I paused. "Sanj has always really wanted a giant evil elephant."

"Urgh, urgh, urgh, urgh, urgh, urgh," Igor said.

"Oh, I like that plan. Take over an abandoned sunken ship and build your lair there. Shark guards and everything. Cool," I said. "What are you going to do, Geeky Girl?"

"I've thought about converting a bunch of old disused space satellites that are orbiting the Earth into a recycled space station. So I guess I could just call it an evil lair," she said.

"With laser defenses and, like, a satellite-enhanced cloaking system too, I suppose," I added.

"Um, yeah, maybe," she said. "And you?"

"I have the best plan." I smiled. "It's an evil lair inside someone else's evil lair."

"What?" she said. "You mean take over someone else's lair?"

"No, run a completely secret lair inside someone else's lair. Unknown to them. It's protected by all their defenses and hidden by all their anti-lair detection devices, but it's known only to me. And the best bit is it's cheap to run too. The other evil guy will be paying all the electricity and laser bills already. And if he bugs me or I just need more room, then I can always take over his evil lair from within."

"Urgh." Igor nodded and patted me on the back.

"Yeah, it is genius. We better go and get ready for the luau tonight," I said, scooping up Fang.

"We have Tahitian dance practice before," Geeky Girl said, and slumped back onto the bed.

"See you there," I said as we left.

"Urgh." Igor waved.

"We'll try to scare away some of the fans outside your tent as we go," I said. "This should be fun..."

As I opened Geeky Girl's tent flap I shouted, "He's been infected by the bite of the jelly-brain tick and his brain has turned to jelly! Watch out!"

Then Igor burst out of the tent and flailed around, and shouted "Urghy, urghy, urghy!"

Campers ran screaming.

It was good.

"See ya later!" I shouted back to Geeky Girl as Igor and I walked back to our tent with him yelling "Urghy!" occasionally at people as we passed.

5

When Igor and I arrived at dance practice the drums were booming, Kirsty was trying to teach everyone some kind of weird kicking move and Geeky Girl was nowhere to be seen.

Kirsty shouted to us, "You two! You're late!"

"Um, sorry," I lied, but I was actually thinking that I wished I had been late enough to miss this whole thing.

The drumbeat was fast and furious, and the movements kept changing. I mean, I am not a bad dancer. I can move. My grandmother once made me learn the polka so I could dance with her at my cousin's wedding, and I totally rocked that polka. Grandma had to see her chiropractor after the wedding, but she said she'd had a good time.

Anyway, the point is, I'm OK at this dancing thing, but my feet and my hips just didn't get Tahitian dancing. Compared to Igor, though, I was Fred Astaire (who I totally know is the dancing tuxedo guy from movies my grandma watches).

Geeky Girl finally slumped into the rehearsal. She stood at the back, but Kirsty called her up to demonstrate something. "Your grandmother sent over this special grass skirt for you to wear tonight," she said, handing Geeky Girl the skirt.

It was just like earlier. Everyone had these fake smiles on their faces when they talked to Geeky Girl. I had a real smile on my face from watching Igor trying to dance, so the only one without a smile was Geeky Girl. She should be happy as a kitten with string, but she looked like someone had just stepped on her new grass skirt. That's when I stepped on her new grass skirt.

"Ouch. Hey, watch it, Mark," she grumbled.

"Sorry, I can't get the hang of this dance," I said. "You look like your budgie died. Snap out of it. I know that this dance practice thing is pretty pathetic." I looked around and caught a glimpse of Sanj attempting to shake his hips in a way that I never need to see again. "OK, this dance thing is super pathetic, but there's a luau party tonight with your epic evil gran. You could at least smile about that."

"I guess," she said, still not smiling at all. "I gotta go work on my lair design. I'll see you tonight," she said, and snuck out of the dancing.

Pretty soon night fell and the torches were lit. The luau was set up, we all had on Tahitian leis and Madame Mako sat at the head of a big bamboo table.

As we all assembled, the counselors got up to make a couple of announcements and to get things started.

Trevor spoke first, "Ve are pleased to velcome Madame Mako here to camp, and she is looking forvard to seeing your evil lair designs. Just some announcements. First, zere has been a report of something called jelly-brain ticks in the area, so be careful."

Igor and I did a quiet low five.

"Second, I vant to remind you zat we will continue to do regular illegal-pet inspections. Pets zat are hibernating still count as pets. Zey are still illegal.

"Zird, just a reminder zat ze loser of zis week's contest vill be sent home in ze Canoe of Shame (assuming zey survive, zat is).

"And fourth, I just vanted to say how particularly evil our little star camper Geeky Girl is looking zis evening."

Geeky Girl was just sneaking in the back, wearing her normal, really-not-evil-at-all T-shirt and jeans but with an even-less-evil grass skirt over the top of it.

Igor waved and pointed to the seat next to us that we had saved for her.

All eyes turned and looked at Geeky Girl as Madame Mako motioned for her to come and sit by her side at the table. Geeky Girl took the long walk with the whole camp staring at her every grassy swish on her way to the table.

I looked over at her, caught her eye and did a little mock royal hand wave. After all, she was totally evil royalty. Now I just had to get Madame Mako to realize that although I'm not related to her, I am totally an unrecognized evil genius waiting to be discovered. I mimed putting on a crown and smiled. Geeky Girl rolled her eyes and slumped into her seat.

Madame Mako clapped her hands and the music started.

One by one, we all got up and presented our evil lair plans to Madame Mako.

I think she liked mine. Although she still had her "not impressed with anything" face on. She did say, "I like the way you plan for betrayal." Which was creepy but pretty positive, right?

As Sanj got up to do his presentation, I whispered, "Option A or Option B?"

He turned. "A hybrid of the two." He smiled.

"So, my evil lair," he said to Madame Mako, showing her his design plans, "would be a constantly moving lair that would be impossible to detect. It would be camouflaged by a prototype teleportation field that kept it slightly out of sync with our current time and space, and it would be on the back of a giant evil elephant."

Then she smiled. She actually smiled. She smiled at Sanj's design? And at the elephant?

What was she thinking?

"I like the tech, don't get me wrong, but you are chasing disaster with the giant-evil-elephant plan," she said. "I myself have been trying to breed giant evil elephants for years, but I discovered that the gene that makes them large also makes them more cuddly. A giant evil elephant is a genetic impossibility, I'm afraid." She shook her head. "But I like the way you think." She paused. "Next."

Bob and Diablo both had really cool lairs planned. I was actually impressed. Diablo's was shaped like a giant wrestling ring and was guarded by evil costumed professional wrestlers. And Bob's was an evil lair disguised as a tour bus for a heavy metal group that was called "Evil Lair." How cool is that?

Soon everyone had presented their plans and the Tahitian dancing began. We had practiced for what seemed like hours, and I could just not get it. Geeky Girl was OK. Igor was very good at the stomping, but I'm pretty sure that he is built without hips. He just kinda hinges at the waist. There is literally no side-to-side movement possible. But he can do the stomping.

Looking at the dancing, Madame Mako's face went from "not impressed" to "seriously in pain at being made to sit through this." She looked like she was about to get up to leave when Dustin and Goth Girl, or Ezmirelda, took to the stage. They were amazing.

Dustin had this kinda Irish-dancing-meets-hip-hop-meets-Tahitian-luau thing going on. It sounds weird, but it actually worked. And Ezmirelda just danced really, really evilly. I mean, she did the same swaying and stomping that we were all taught this afternoon, but she did it with serious evil intent. It rocked.

Madame Mako stood and clapped. Then she held up her hand again and the music stopped.

"I am hungry," she said. "Have those two who danced, the elephant-lair boy, the wresting-lair boy and the rock-group-lair boy join me at my table with my granddaughter and her two henchmen." She paused. "That is all. Eat."

I looked at Igor. "I think she means us," I said, and walked over to the table.

"We seriously have to get over this 'henchmen' thing. We need her to see us as top evil geniuses in the making." I straightened my shirt to look more dignified. "We gotta look the part."

Igor smoothed his monobrow and looked serious.

"Yeah, good. That's it," I said.

Geeky Girl was really quiet while we ate. I mean she isn't, like, always chatty or anything, but she just sat next to her grandmother and didn't say a word.

As we ate, Madame Mako reached down and unclipped Lucky from his chain. He wagged his tail and stood up. "Go do your business, Lucky," she said, and he trotted off toward the woods.

"Is that safe?" Geeky Girl asked Madame Mako. "I mean, what if he meets a camper on the way to go dragon pee in the woods?"

"Then they shouldn't have left the luau, should they?" she answered without looking up from her stew.

Igor pulled on my white coat under the table so the others couldn't see, and then he tilted his head to the side to point.

"What are you trying to say, Igor?" I whispered.

Then Igor mimed what looked like a bird flapping in that direction, followed by a kitten stalking the bird.

"But we left them in the tent?! Did you see them head that way?" I asked.

Igor nodded.

That's when we heard what sounded like a bird screech followed by a hiss.

6

I stood up from the table. "Ummmm, I think I have to . . . ummm . . . you know . . . ummm . . . in the woods too." I started to run for the woods.

I followed the sound of the hissing, hoping for once that it was just a snake and not my evil vampire kitten battling a big old Komodo dragon, but of course I'm never that lucky. Especially, it seems, with Lucky.

I saw Boris first. He was sitting on a branch looking down into a ditch. There were Lucky and Fang, circling each other. Lucky's tongue shot in and out of his mouth tasting the air. Fang's fur stood on end and she was arched in the middle like a Halloween cat ready to fight.

One of Lucky's claws was the size of her whole body, but she did not look like she was going to back down.

I swear if Godzilla had walked into Camp Mwhaaa-haa-ha-a-watha, Fang would find a reason to pick a fight with him. Why does she think she needs to fight every creature that crosses her path?

I tried to distract Fang. I took off my lei and dragged it in front of her like a string. She is a sucker for a string usually, but she just ignored the dangling loop of flowers and stared right into Lucky's dark, cold eyes. I tossed the lei aside. "OK, that didn't work. Come on, kitten. Let's go."

"REeeeoowwworrrllll." She did that kitten growl thing that means "I'm taking you down." Lucky responded by inflating his throat and then letting out a deep, loud, mean "HIIIIISSSSS" that went on for ages. If I spoke Komodo (which I don't), I would totally think he'd said, "Yeah, in your dreams, fur ball."

"Just walk away, Fang," I mumbled. "Good evil

kitten, fight another day. Just walk away." Lucky
lurched toward Fang and hissed again. "OK,
change of plans: just run, kitten. RUN!" I shouted.

I tried chucking sticks at Lucky to distract
him and get him to chase me instead, but they just
bounced off. I looked at Boris. "Go get help!" I
said.

He fluttered off back toward the camp.

I managed to find a long, thick forked stick and
tried to use it to hold Lucky back by his shoulders
so that Fang could make a sprint for it. She didn't
twitch, though.

"Come on, Fang. You can't take this dragon. Run," I shouted, but she wouldn't back down.

Then they stopped circling. They stared each other down. I braced myself and pushed on the stick, trying to force Lucky to back up. He was solid muscle, though. I could barely hold him still, let alone push him back. Then he turned quickly and flicked his tail against the stick, freeing himself. He reared up and slammed down on it like a World Wrestling Entertainment champ. The thick stick snapped like a twig. There was nothing to stop him now.

Then we heard the whistle and "Heel, Lucky." Madame Mako sat on a chair carried by Igor,

 and snapped her fingers. Then she elbowed Igor. "That means 'set me down,'" she scolded.

"Urgh, urgh," Igor mumbled as he placed the chair on the ground.

As Lucky trotted

back to Madame Mako's side like nothing had happened, she continued to stare at me and Fang.

Geeky Girl ran up behind them with Boris fluttering ahead of her. "What happened?" she said. "Boris looked like he wanted us to follow him. Kirsty and Phillipe wanted to come with us when they saw us leaving, but I told them my grandmother wanted to see the woods on her own. They listened to me! Kirsty even curtsied again. It was weird."

"Yeah, that's weird," I said. "But kinda cool."

"Anyway, are you OK?" she said to me.

"Yeah," I said. "But Fang was nearly dragon food."

"Meeeeooooowwwlll," Fang meowed, and jumped out of the pit, still staring down Lucky.

"Is that yours?" Madame Mako said, pointing at Fang. Fang hissed again, this time at Madame Mako and moved like she was going to pounce.

"Easy, girl," I said, scratching her ear as I scooped her up. "She is with me," I said.

Then Madame Mako looked at Geeky Girl.

"That is an example of an evil pet that shows some promise," she said. "At least it's brave."

Boris fluttered off Geeky Girl's shoulder and headed back to camp.

"Urgh, urgh, urgh," Igor muttered.

"Yeah, I think his feelings were hurt too," I said.

"Your henchmen were also brave," Madame Mako said.

"Um, thanks, but you got it wrong with the whole henchmen thing. We're our own evil scientists actually," I said.

"Yeah, they aren't my—" Geeky Girl started to say, but Madame Mako had stopped listening.

"Granddaughter, why don't you come back and stay at the island tonight. There are so many things we haven't discussed."

Geeky Girl looked over at me.

"I should check on . . ." Geeky Girl started.

"Igor and I can check on Boris," I said. "He'll be sulking, but he'll be fine." I mouthed the words "Go, it's your grandma" to her.

Geeky Girl shrugged her shoulders and nodded. "OK," she said.

Then I whispered, "And if you could mention that we aren't your henchmen and we are actually very hardworking, clever . . ."

"Urgh, urgh," Igor whispered too.

"Yeah, and brave, young evil scientists who might be great to one day take over a floating volcano island, then that would be great too," I added.

Madame Mako snapped her fingers again. "Up!" she commanded.

Igor shrugged and lifted the chair once again.

"To the bridge," she said to Igor, and they headed off to the volcano island with Lucky trotting along behind.

I scooped up Fang and headed back to camp. "I'll see you at the tent, Igor!" I shouted after them.

"Urgh," he answered.

I stroked Fang as we walked back. "OK, that lady is hard to impress. We faced down her Komodo dragon, and all we got is that we were kinda brave," I said. "We need to show her our total epicness, Fang. And we need to be ready if we have to square off with that dragon again. Luckily, I am ace at epic evil plans. We better get started." When we got back to the tent, we found Boris sitting on the branch above our door.

"Thanks, Boris. You saved us by getting help," I said. "Come on, I'll keep Fang away from you and get you some cookie crumbs or something."

He fluttered in after us.

When I had given Boris some crumbs and Fang had licked out the insides of three of my grandma's peanut butter sandwich cookies, Igor stomped back into the tent.

"Urgh, urgh, urgh," he muttered.

"I know you're nobody's henchman, Igor," I said. "And so does Geeky Girl. You are your own evil scientist, dude. Still, thanks for bringing her over to call off the dragon. I thought Fang and I were dragon food out there."

Boris fluttered down and landed on Igor's shoulder.

"Oh, yeah, Geeky Girl is staying on the island tonight with her grandmother, Boris, so I guess you can stay here with us if you want? You just have to keep out of sight . . . ," I started to say, but Boris flapped up and headed for the tent flap to leave. He motioned for us to follow.

"You don't like her being there without you, Boris?" I asked.

Fang meowed and hissed at the lei from the luau that was hanging around Igor's neck. She tore it off him and shredded it in seconds.

"I don't thing Fang trusts Madame Mako much either," I said.

Boris fluttered down and landed on my shoulder.

"It's a shame we can't all go over there and see what's going on," I said.

Igor mimed the bridge to the island being pulled back as soon as Madame Mako and Geeky Girl had crossed over onto the flying island.

"So hard for us to get across, but not for Boris,"

I said. "Maybe he can spy on Madame Mako and let us know if there's trouble."

Then Igor got that look like a giant Igor-size lightbulb was going off in his head. He rushed over to the trunk by his bed with his stuff in it and pulled out a small camera attached to a head strap.

"Even better!" I said. "We can see what Boris sees. You up for being an evil spy, Boris?" I said.

He shook his head.

"OK, a non-evil spy then. Come on," I said.

We fixed the camera to Boris's head and sent him off toward the island. Soon Bob and Diablo came back from the luau and we all turned off our flashlights and went to sleep. Well, we went to bed.

I had the camera monitor under my pillow, and Fang was hiding under the covers. Igor and I each had one of the earbuds in our ears to hear what they were saying too.

Geeky Girl and her grandmother were walking around the outside of the volcano lair and talking. With them outside, it made it easy for Boris to flutter close by and eavesdrop on the conversation.

"I'm so pleased that you are doing so well at Evil Scientist Camp. I have been following your progress here with interest. When I heard that you were following in the family tradition, my heart jumped for joy. It was not a stress-related palpitation like the doctors said," she added.

"Are you having heart problems, Grandmother?" Geeky Girl asked.

"My doctors say that the stress of being a celebrity evil scientist has taken its toll. They think I should retire for my health. It's not easy running an evil empire. It's a job for the young," she said, patting Geeky Girl's shoulder. "It's a shame your mother never wanted to take over the business. I could have retired years ago."

"You offered Mom your evil empire?" Geeky Girl asked. "But she never mentioned it. Or that this is what you did."

"Your mother was embarrassed by all this. She moved continents and married that man who sold newspapers to get away from her inheritance," Madame Mako said.

"Mom is very happy," Geeky Girl said, "except when she talks about you. I think she wishes that you visited more. She was very excited to go see you this summer in Tahiti while I was at camp," she said.

"I asked your mother a final time when she visited if she would take over the empire, but she said no. I thought you could run it together as mother and daughter, but she said she was raising you NOT to be evil." Madame Mako shook her head. "We had nothing further to say.

"You can imagine how thrilled I was, then, when I heard about your progress here. You are following in my footsteps after all. I can teach you all you need to know to run a truly great evil empire. You can even bring along your henchmen if you like," she said.

"They're not my henchmen," Geeky Girl corrected. "They're their own hardworking, evil, clever, um, what was the other thing? Oh yeah, brave evil scientists," she said. "And they're my friends."

"Urgh, urgh, urgh," Igor said, and sniffled.

"You are not allowed to get sniffly over that, big man. That is soooo not an evil-enough thing to say," I whispered. "But she'll learn, and she did get all the other stuff in about us. Result."

Igor and I leaned across the beds and high-fived.

"She is being given the keys to the volcano," I said.

"Urgh, urgh, urgh?" Igor asked.

"I don't know if there are actual keys," I said. "I mean, Madame Mako is basically asking her to run her evil empire when she retires, and we could run it with her!" Geeky Girl was being offered the opportunity of a lifetime. This is what Igor wanted. This is what I wanted. I think this is even what Fang wanted! (Especially if it meant she got to boss around that Komodo dragon.)

Then Madame Mako spoke again. "Henchmen are more valuable than friends," she said. "But we can come back to that. So, do you accept my offer?"

Geeky Girl paused.

"Grandma, I don't know if that's what I want," she said. "What if I don't want to run an evil empire? What if I don't even want to be an evil scientist? Maybe I just want to be a regular scientist." She paused again. "No, scratch that. I want to be an extraordinary scientist, but maybe just not an evil one."

"Then why are you here?" Madame Mako asked.

"It was a mistake. It's kinda a long story. I'm getting cold. Can we go inside?" she said.

They walked up a ramp to a door, and Boris tried to follow. He was inside, hovering behind the door, and we could see Madame Mako and Geeky Girl disappear around a corner. Just as Boris looked as if he would follow, we heard that horrible slurping sound. Lucky!

We could see the camera shaking as Boris flew up and down trying to avoid claws. Boris levitated higher to get past Lucky's reach, but his tail is long. We could hear a *thwack* as the end of Lucky's tail came into view. We saw a flutter of green feathers and then the camera fell off Boris's head, hit the floor and shattered.

Igor and I both sat up in bed.

"Urgh, urgh, urgh?" Igor asked.

Diablo rolled over in his bed and grunted.

"Shhhhh," I whispered to Igor. "It's OK. Boris could have gotten away," I said. "It doesn't mean Lucky definitely got him. Boris is a tricky bird, and he should be able outmaneuver Lucky . . . Still we don't have any way to know unless we check."

"Urgh, urgh, urgh, urgh," Igor urgh-whispered.

"Yeah, you're right. Geeky Girl will totally kill us if we let Boris get caught by Lucky when we are supposed to be looking out for him. Especially as we actually sent him to spy on her and her grandma instead," I said softly. "We have to get inside the volcano island!"

8

"We just need a few things to help us while we're over there," I said, and grabbed my backpack.

I quietly went over to my trunk of special evil scientist gadgets and inventions that I'd brought from home specifically for this kind of mission (I'm calling this mission "Operation Budgie") and stocked up on a few items we might need.

"OK, we are good to go, Igor," I whispered.

Igor and I snuck out of the tent with Fang. We headed to the edge of the lake. I spotted some canoes on the shore and we quickly climbed in and started to row to the island.

On the other side, we covered the canoe with palm leaves to camouflage it. I reached into my backpack and pulled out my Invisible Lair Trap

Detector and scanned the area. "That's funny," I said. "She has built this massive high-tech volcano lair, and we just rock up on a canoe and aren't lasered or laughing-gassed or anything? It doesn't seem right."

"Urgh, urgh, urgh," Igor said.

"Yeah, maybe Madame Mako got distracted talking to Geeky Girl and didn't switch on her security traps tonight. Come on. It's clear anyway. Let's go."

We ran to the front door—a big, thick metal door in a stone frame. Shut. There was no Boris,

though, and no Lucky. I checked the door to see if we could pick the lock with something or pry it open.

"Urgh," Igor mumbled, and I turned to see him pick up the smashed camera from the floor and a green feather.

"They both must have gotten inside before the door closed. We can't get in this way. We'll just have to find another way in," I said.

"Urgh." Igor pointed up the volcano.

"I guess that's where we go, then," I said, and we started to climb the volcano.

Halfway up, Igor pointed down at the lake. We could see Dustin and Sanj rowing across in another canoe. They must have been spying on us and seen us sneak out of our tent and take the canoe. Spying on us spying. That's pretty low. They probably thought we were trying to impress Madame Mako by breaking into her own lair.

"We don't have time to try and stop them—we have to get to Boris," I said to Igor. "He might be a dragon snack by now."

Just as we climbed to the next ledge of the
volcano, we saw something a little out of place.
There was an open window.

A window that looked like it would be in some
white wood-paneled house in the suburbs was
on the side of the volcano. Who has a window
in a volcano lair? And who leaves a window in a
volcano lair wide open?

"Urgh?" Igor asked.

"I don't know," I said, "but it looks like a way in.
Let's go."

We clambered in through the window and
dropped silently to the floor below. Well, I
dropped silently—Igor kinda thudded not so
silently.

We could hear voices at the end of the corridor

and followed them. It sounded like Geeky Girl
and Madame Mako, but they didn't sound upset
or anything. Maybe she didn't know about Lucky
attacking Boris. We headed for the room.

A few yards away from the door, a face poked
its head around the corner. A large dribbling lizard
face. It spotted us, and Lucky charged.

Fang jumped down in front of us in attack
kitten stance and held her ground, hissing as the
dragon stampeded in our direction. I reached
into my backpack and pulled out one of my secret
inventions, Insta-Sticky Anti-Animal-Attack Spray.

I aimed and sprayed at Lucky and caught him on his front claws. It slowed him as he started to stick to the floor, but didn't stop him. One dragon-head away, Lucky was yanked back by his golden chain. It was slightly too short for him to reach us.

Just as we let ourselves breathe again and turned to try to tiptoe away, a voice called out, "You had better come in, then. Both of you," Madame Mako said. Then she whistled and Lucky trotted back out to the corridor. His Insta-Sticky-Spray-covered claws slurped on the floor like suction cups being pulled up with every step.

Fang jumped back into my pocket as we entered the room, and we could see that Madame Mako and Geeky Girl both sat at a long dining table. The room was like a massive cave but decorated with elegant chandeliers, and long fabric tapestries covered the walls. Boris fluttered over to Geeky Girl's shoulder.

"Oh right," I said. "So, if Boris is OK and not dragon food, then we'll just be going . . ."

"Sit," Madame Mako said.

We sat.

"You were spying on me? You were using my own budgie to spy on me?" Geeky Girl said.

"To be fair it was kinda Boris's idea," I said, and Igor nodded.

Lucky sat under the table and licked at his feet. "What is that on my dragon?" Madame Mako asked.

"Insta-Sticky Anti-Animal-Attack Spray," I said. "Raspberry flavor," I added.

"Ahhh," she said. "He seems to like it." Lucky got up and headed out of the room again and Madame Mako turned back to us.

"So, my plan is panning out perfectly. We'll just wait for the others."

"What others?" Geeky Girl said.

Just then Sanj and Dustin were herded into the room by Lucky.

"We were expecting you," Madame Mako said, and gestured to the empty seats.

"I really wasn't," Geeky Girl added.

"I was. We saw you in the canoes. You were following us," I said.

"Urgh, urgh," Igor said.

"Igor actually forgot that you were here but then remembered when you came in," I translated.

"It was easy to get in with that open window," Sanj said.

"Of course it was," I said.

"You put an open window in a volcano lair, Grandma?" Geeky Girl asked.

"Yes, and it worked well for letting in precisely who I wanted to be let in," Madame Mako replied. "Now wait."

"Um, excuse me, what are we waiting for?" Sanj asked.

"The others," Madame Mako said.

Then Bob and Diablo were brought in by Lucky.

"OK, I seriously was not expecting that," I said.

"We were following Sanj and Dustin," Bob said. "And there was this open window . . ."

Everyone nodded.

"You don't get to run an evil empire for half a century without being in control. This is all going to my plan. Just a few more to arrive," she said.

"Who else could possibly be coming?" Sanj asked.

He was interrupted by the doorbell ringing.

Lucky went to the front door to answer and came back with Trevor, Kirsty and Phillipe.

"We received your message, Madame Mako," Phillipe said, looking around at the assembled campers. Boris quietly fluttered out of sight up into the rafters of the room.

It was then I noticed that Fang was no longer in

my pocket. She must have slipped out while we were sitting here and I didn't feel it. But where could she be?

"Nearly ready," Madame Mako said. "One more."

Just then we heard a crash of a window breaking in the corridor.

9

Lucky rushed out and came back into the room with Ezmirelda.

"Oh, now I totally didn't see that coming," I said.

"Why didn't you just use the open window?" Bob asked.

"That's way too obvious," she snarled.

"You have to know your audience," Madame Mako said. "For some, an open window is an invitation to come in; for others a closed window is an invitation to burst through ninja style." She smiled and motioned for the others to sit.

"Now you are all here." She sat down.

"I feel like I'm in a murder mystery or something," Geeky Girl said.

"Don't worry, no one will be murdered tonight. Unless Lucky takes a dislike to you for some reason," Madame Mako added.

"That doesn't sound too good for us," I mumbled to Igor.

"I am not a person who believes in wasting time. I don't want to go through several tedious days in your camp when I had identified the finalists for my challenge already. I thought it was simpler to bring you all here with the camp counselors to ensure it is all in order and just in case one of you falls off the volcano, gets consumed by lava or just eaten by Lucky here."

Lucky burped on cue.

"I have set a game around the volcano to test your skills. There are clues and there are traps, and the person to complete the tasks and get to the top of the volcano first wins this little Evil Emperor of the Week thing you people seem to care about but also might win the right to join my evil empire and shadow me before I retire," she said, looking directly at Geeky Girl.

No pressure, then.

"You have all proved yourselves in some way, so you all have a chance," she added.

"Just to be clear. Will there be a crown awarded to the winner?" I said.

Madame Mako completely blanked me. She picked up a large hourglass and turned it over. "You have one hour. Begin."

I looked around, and everyone started for the door. Bob and Diablo were out first, followed by Ezmirelda and Sanj and Dustin.

"Urgh, urgh!" Igor shouted from the door.

"I'm coming!" I shouted back. It was as I stood up that I saw where Fang had gone.

She was hanging batlike directly over Madame Mako's head. She must have climbed up behind the tapestries and slunk along the light fittings until she was in prime attack position. As the camp counselors and the last of the kids, except for Igor, left the room, she was getting ready to pounce on Madame Mako.

From where Madame Mako stood, Fang was inches away from the netted bun on top of her head. Then in one super swift motion of her hand Madame Mako removed the dagger pinning her hair, loosened the hair net, swung it upward and netted Fang. Fang dangled in the net hanging from her hair dagger.

"So, the old hang-upside-down-like-a-stealth-bat-and-catch-the-victim-unaware-when-they-stand trick." Madame Mako yawned. "I expected something better, little evil one." She looked at Fang, all netted up and squirming.

"I believe this belongs to you," she said, sliding the net of angry kitten from the hilt of the weapon. Fang sliced through the bag and jumped onto the table facing Madame Mako. Boris flew down and hovered over Fang's head. They both glared at Madame Mako.

"Fang and Boris," I said in a voice that sounded scarily like a teacher whose student had just written *My Evil Vampire Pet ate my homework* on the whiteboard. (Not that I would know what that sounds like.)

I cleared my throat and used my regular voice again. "I get that you're mad, but we have one hour, and you're wasting time. I need to get that crown!" I paused. "And I might need your help, Fang, so come on."

Geeky Girl walked up to her grandmother. "I'm not sure what you want me to do," she said.

"I want you to win, Glenda. But I also want you to realize that you can win and you can do this on your own. You are capable of leading this empire—with a bit of advice from your grandmother." Madame Mako smiled. "Now, you are the one wasting time. The clock is ticking."

"Urgh, urgh, urgh," Igor said.

"Yeah, I think she knows that hourglasses don't actually tick. I think it's just an expression and she means, 'We gotta get a move on.' Geeky Girl, are you coming?" I said, scooping up Fang from the table and putting her in my white coat pocket.

She looked back at her grandma. "Yes," she said, and we ran out of the room with Boris flying behind us.

I got out my Invisible Lair Trap Detector and scanned the corridor. "Jump now," I said, and illuminated the laser trip wire on the floor. "Duck!" I shouted as a heavy log swung down over us, and we flattened ourselves on the floor.

We stood up. "OK, it's clear," I said. "So, what are we looking for, anyway?"

"Clues, messages, something that looks out of place," Geeky Girl said.

"Urgh." Igor pointed to a wall.

"Yeah, like that, Igor," Geeky Girl said. "That Tahitian mask is hanging upside down."

"Then we fix it," I said, and turned the mask.

The mask released a panel in the floor and it suddenly gave way under us. Before I knew it, we were hurtling down a giant slide. "OK, that maybe wasn't what I wanted to do."

10

Igor hit the bottom first, and then we all crashed down on top of him.

"Right, so we have a bit farther to go up now, I guess," Geeky Girl said.

"We just need to find the stairs. Or an elevator maybe," I said. I started opening doors in the room we fell into, looking for a way out.

Geeky Girl opened a door, and it had a sliding gate behind it like you get in old-style apartment elevators. "I think I found something," she said. "And there's a plaque on the door. It says, 'Aim high if you want to succeed, but always check you have what you need.'"

"So," I said, getting into the elevator with Igor and Geeky Girl, "it says 'aim high.' There's a button marked 'penthouse.' That must be at the top of the volcano."

"Did you see a penthouse at the top of the volcano?" Geeky Girl asked.

"Urgh, urgh, urgh," Igor said.

"Good point. If she puts an open window and an elevator in, then maybe there is a penthouse," I said, and I pressed the button.

The floor of the elevator disappeared and again we found ourselves sliding down a chute to an even lower floor.

THUD, thud, thud. We all crashed down into a corridor in a different part of the volcano.

"We are wasting time," Geeky Girl said. "We're supposed to be going up! To get to the top of the volcano."

"But the clue said to aim high, and we did," I said.

"Yes, but the clue also said to check that you have what you need," Geeky Girl said. "Maybe we needed to bring something with us from before."

"Well, nice to know that now," I said, kicking my foot against the wall. It was then that I noticed the floor. We were standing on a square that said "Back to the Start."

"OK, think I found another clue," I said.

"Yes!" Geeky Girl said. "We have to go back to the start. We have to get back to that mask. It's where we began. Maybe we need something from that. We have to start over."

"Urgh?" Igor said.

Fang jumped out of my pocket and began to sniff around the square with the writing. Then she pounced on the word *Start*.

A rope ladder dropped from the ceiling.

"I guess it wants us to go up this time," Geeky Girl said.

Fang climbed up the ladder, followed by me,

Igor and Geeky Girl with Boris fluttering behind.

It led us right back to the corridor and the mask.

"OK, we need to take something from here. There is something we need," Geeky Girl said.

Boris landed on the mask and pecked at its eye. "Careful, Boris, that might be an antique or something," Geeky Girl said. But Boris kept pecking. Soon he dislodged what looked like an ornate metal key from the mask.

"OK, if we're starting over, I know what do to next," I said, and turned the mask.

"Woo-hoo!" Geeky Girl shouted as we all slid down into the room from before.

"Urgh, urgh, urgh," Igor said.

"I know, dude, it's all very up and down. Maybe, now that we have the key, from here it will just be up," I said.

We headed straight to the elevator and looked for a keyhole. Sure enough there was one that said "loft" underneath it.

"That must be it," Geeky Girl said, placing the key in the slot and pressing the button. But instead of moving up, the ceiling of the elevator dropped down another ladder.

"Hang on," Geeky Girl said. "This is Chutes and Ladders! We're playing Chutes and Ladders. I remember the one time that my grandma came to visit when I was very little, she brought us this game. We played for hours. It's her favorite."

"So, she made a volcano into a giant Chutes and Ladders game?" I asked. "Great, how do we win?"

"You just avoid the chutes and climb the ladders, I guess. I'm assuming the clues will tell us the rest," she said.

Boris and Fang didn't wait for us. They were

up the ladder in no time. When we got to the top, we were in a room with ten doors. A square on the floor said, "Add the letters in your name. Then you'll know the door to claim. Quickly now, and don't waste time. I can't believe I have to make all these rhyme."

"So, does it mean that you have to add the number of letters in your name? OK, let's try. Igor, do you want to go first?" I said.

He counted *I, G, O, R* and went to Door Four. He knocked four times, and it opened and a ladder dropped. Igor started to climb.

"OK, we got this," Geeky Girl said. "Boris, you go next."

Boris went to Door Five. He tapped his beak five times, and the door opened and a ladder dropped. He flew up by the ladder.

"OK, I'll go next," she said.

I went to pick up Fang so she could go after. I wasn't paying attention to see what door Geeky Girl went to. She went to Door Nine and knocked. As soon as she did, the floor opened and she slid down a chute.

I'd stood at Door Four, but had only tapped in the *F* from Fang's name when I'd gotten distracted by Geeky Girl. Before I could finish tapping in the other letters, the floor opened up under me, and Fang and I tumbled down the chute as well.

We slid down for what seemed like ages before we hit the bottom.

"I was getting to it!" I shouted up the chute from the bottom. "Wow, it really doesn't give you much time. What if you're a slow counter?" I added.

"Grrr!" Geeky Girl shouted. "Why didn't that work for me, then?"

"Because you did the number for Geeky Girl, and your grandmother calls you Glenda," I said. "Now we have to get out of here and catch up to Igor and Boris."

We looked around the room. It was darker than the other rooms and colder.

"Are we in the basement?" Geeky Girl said.

I looked at the square on the floor. There was nothing on it. There was nothing on the walls or the floor, just a sticker that said "Quality Assured, Manufactured by Impenetrable Plastics 'R' Us."

And then an exit sign illuminated above the door.

"So, I guess we go out here?" I said, and started for the door.

"Wait!" Geeky Girl shouted.

Then I saw that Geeky Girl was staring at the sign. It switched back and forth from "Lose" to "Exit."

11

"I think we lost. I think this is how we leave the game when we lose. The way out to go back to camp and wait to see who gets to train as my grandma's successor," she said.

"And see who gets the crown?" I said. "My crown."

"It looks like the only way out," she said. "We lost."

"You're giving up? Just like that?" I asked. "Well, I'm not. I am not on the Canoe of Shame this week. There's gotta be another way out."

"I don't even want to be in charge of my grandmother's empire. That's what you want," Geeky Girl said.

"Of course I want it!" I said. "I mean, I think it's

like the best evil dream job ever! Your grandma thinks I'm just a henchman, so I gotta prove to her that I'm strong enough and smart enough to run this place. And I'm gonna do that. Madame Mako already thinks you can run her empire, but maybe you gotta prove to yourself that you're strong enough and smart enough to do it. If you don't want this—like, really don't want it—then that's fine. Walk out that exit door. But if you're quitting because you think you can't do it, then that's another thing."

Fang jumped out of my pocket and started sniffing around the bit of wall where the slide dumped us out. It had closed again behind us,  but you could see there was an edge where the trapdoor opened. An edge that was just big enough for an evil kitten to slip a claw through and swipe.

The door slid open again, revealing a long, long slide up to the room with the ten doors.

"I don't think Fang's ready to lose just yet," I said. "How about you?"

"But ladders are up and chutes are down. That's how the game works," Geeky Girl said.

"Then, in the time-honored tradition of evil scientists—we cheat," I said.

I got the Insta-Sticky Anti-Animal-Attack Spray and sprayed it onto both Geeky Girl's and my hands and feet and onto Fang's paws. "That ought to help us get some traction for the climb," I said, and started up the chute.

Now, I don't know if you have ever climbed up a slide in the park when you were little or climbed a doorway Spider-Man style. It was kinda like that, but I made it a little bit easier with the sticky spray. Slowly, we climbed up and up, until eventually we made it to the room with the ten doors.

Geeky Girl went to Door Six for

Glenda; Fang went to Door Four, and I followed right behind her.

Fang waited for me on a rung of the ladder, and then jumped into my pocket once I got through, and we climbed. The ladders led up to what looked like a walkway around the crater of the volcano with several bridges that led out to a room in the middle.

There just outside the room were Igor, Boris, Dustin, Sanj, Bob and Diablo.

"We were wondering if you were going to make it through," Sanj said. "I had said you probably wouldn't."

"Urgh, urgh, urgh, urgh," Igor added.

"Yeah, I know you would have my back," I said to Igor.

"Does anybody else think it's weird that there's this bird that's following us too?" Diablo added. I made sure Fang was hidden inside my pocket out of sight.

"Maybe it's a spy for Madame Mako?"

Bob asked. "It could be, like, reporting back on how we're doing." Bob started swatting at Boris, but Igor blocked his hand.

"Urgh, urgh, urgh," he said.

"Yeah, good call, Igor," I said. "You might get disqualified if you swat at the spy bird."

Sanj looked over at Boris. "Don't be ridiculous. That bird belongs to—"

Geeky Girl interrupted. "Possibly my grandmother. And she gets very protective about things that belong to her family."

Sanj gulped. "Yes, probably best to ignore the bird."

Geeky Girl smiled. "I think Grandma would like that," she said.

"So, I guess Goth Girl, I mean Ezmirelda, didn't make it," I said, changing the subject just as the wall next to me started to shake and a drill poked through from the other side. Then a foot kicked out a bigger hole where the drill came out. It was Ezmirelda's foot.

"I missed one of the ladders so I had to find my own way up," she said, climbing through. "Inside the wall."

"Respect," I said as the three of us went out to the center to join the others.

"Oh great, you mean *all* of you made it!" Sanj whined. "Well, this is just far too easy a contest."

Diablo spoke. "Man, I think you're forgetting that none of us have won yet. We have to get into the room without being sent down one of those giant slides."

I looked around and saw that there were

giant tube slides off the central platform that we were standing on. They all had stickers from the Impenetrable Plastics 'R' Us Company too. The slides seemed to head so far down into the volcano that you couldn't see where they came out.

"And once we get in, if we get in, the box in the center of the room is guarded by the Komodo dragon," Dustin added.

We looked inside the glass room at the center of the volcano. Inside, Lucky paced back and forth. He looked grumpy to be stuck in a big glass room in a volcano, and worst of all, he looked hungry.

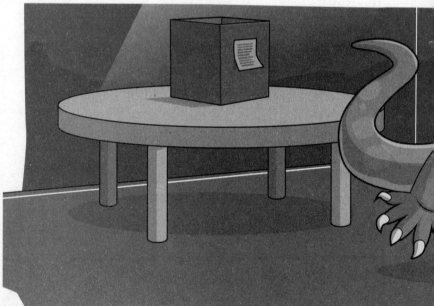

"Urgh, urgh, urgh," Igor agreed.

"Yeah, a couple of big problems there," I said.

"So, is there a clue to figure out?" Geeky Girl said.

Bob passed her the paper that was stuck on the door of the glass room.

"'Music may sooth the savage beast, but if you choose wrong, then you'll be the feast.

"'A good sense of rhythm opens the door, but one false move and you'll slide through the floor,'" Geeky Girl read aloud.

"Have you tried anything yet?" I asked.

"I didn't exactly want to risk becoming a dragon feast or sliding through the floor," Bob said. "So no."

"It sounds like some rhythmic pattern will unlock the door," Geeky Girl said.

"Like this," Ezmirelda said, and started stomping out the dance from the luau. The door started vibrating. "It's not enough!"

Dustin joined in and the two of them shook the floor with their dancing.

"What if this just shakes us off the platform and we fall all the way down into the volcano instead?" I said. "I'm assuming that is not the plan."

As Dustin and Ezmirelda swayed and stomped the last move of the dance the door to the room slid open.

"We're in!" I shouted, just as Lucky turned and noticed that the door was open too.

"Yeah, we're in and he's out!" Bob shouted.

12

Lucky took a step toward us.

"Don't worry," I said, "I've got my Insta-Sticky
Anti-Animal-Attack Spray."

I took out the can, aimed at Lucky and sprayed,
but it just spat out a few strands of raspberry goo.

"We used it all climbing up the slide," Geeky
Girl said.

"So, you climbed up the slides? That's cheating," Ezmirelda added.

"Right, and climbing up through the walls is totally in the rules, right?" Geeky Girl replied.

"It doesn't matter. It's an evil contest. So what do we do now?" Diablo shouted.

"Lucky! Eat him first!" Sanj said to the lizard, pointing to Igor. "He'll fill you up, and you won't need to eat skinny little me."

"Music may sooth the savage beast," Geeky Girl repeated. "Music may sooth the savage beast."

"I know some heavy metal that I can sing to it. I find it kinda soothing," Bob said.

"I could sing 'O Canada,'" Dustin offered.

"Wait! Geeky Girl, is

there a song that your grandma ever sang to you? You know, the whole Chutes and Ladders thing was a memory about you and her—maybe the music is too," I said.

"I hardly knew her. I was a little kid," she said. "I don't remember."

Lucky crept closer and closer. He was swinging his head side to side and using his tongue to taste the air.

"He's trying to figure out who's the best one to start the feast," Diablo said.

"Maybe we could sing Lucky a lullaby," Ezmirelda suggested. "Ya know, like 'Rock-A-Bye Dragon' or 'Twinkle, Twinkle . . .'"

"'Evil Star,'" Geeky Girl mumbled.

"What?" I said.

"'Twinkle, Twinkle, Evil Star'!" she said. "I remember hearing it somewhere. It must have been her. Who else would sing that to a toddler?"

"My mom?" Bob said.

"And mine," Ezmirelda said.

"Urgh, urgh," Igor added.

"OK, yeah, non-evil mom here so regular non-evil lullabies in my house," Geeky Girl said. "But I remember."

"Sing it!" I shouted as Lucky turned and faced me.

Then Geeky Girl started.

"Twinkle, twinkle, evil star,
You're the evilest by far.
Up above my lair so high,
Like a laser in the sky.
Twinkle, twinkle, evil star,
You're the evilest by far."

When she finished, we looked down and Lucky was curled up fast asleep on the floor. And Fang was curled up, snoozing in my pocket. Aha. Now I know how to calm an attacking Komodo dragon or an angry vampire kitten. Even Boris gave a little budgie yawn from Geeky Girl's shoulder.

"Result!" I shouted.

"Shhhhhhhhhh!" everyone whispered. Well, except Igor, who whispered, "Urgh."

"We did it," I whispered. "Yaaaaay," I cheered very, very quietly.

"Well, she mostly did it," Ezmirelda said, pointing to Geeky Girl.

"But now we have to figure out how to finally get out of here," Sanj said.

"There must be something important about the box at the center that Lucky was guarding," Geeky Girl said.

We all gathered around the box.

"Oh great. Another note," Bob said. "Doesn't she get sick of these rhyming notes?"

"'Who'll do the deed that must be done? You've finished now, the race is run. If many choose, then there will be none. For in the end there's only one,'" I read aloud.

Then I read it again because I really didn't get it.

When I read it the third time, Igor took the piece of paper away from me.

"I still don't get it," I said.

"I'm pretty sure it means that there is a task that only one of us can do. Without help. The person has to make the decision and take action on their own," Geeky Girl said.

"I can do that," Ezmirelda said. "What's the task?"

"Hang on, I can do that too." Sanj pushed forward.

"Me too," Diablo said.

"And me." Bob pushed them aside.

"It should be me," Dustin said.

They started pushing one another to get closest to the box. Igor was trying to hold people back.

While the other campers were distracted, Geeky Girl climbed on top of the table and looked inside the box. I climbed up after her. There was a big red button in the box. No explanation. No sign to say what it did. Just a big red button.

"I guess the test is—are you willing to risk everything to press it?" I said.

"Well, it might get us out of here," she said.

"And it might blow up the volcano," I said.

"Ask yourself, WWMMD?" I added.

"What?"

"What Would Madame Mako Do?" I said. "She has a whole section in her words of wisdom book about that. I looked it up. And I think you can even get a key chain with that on it. Anyway, maybe you should think what she would do.

"I can see a lot of you in your grandmother," I said. "See, you're not down there fighting about who is gonna be the leader. You're up here being a leader."

"Then what are you doing?" she asked.

"Ummm, I'm, like, leading the leader toward their leaderness," I said. "And being kinda cool in my own leader-leading leadering."

She stared at me blankly. "OK," I explained, "the clue says that only one of us can do this. I figure your grandmother already thinks you can do this, but I have to prove I should do it. So maybe I should be the one to push the button and win the contest, and then we can run the volcano together, because your grandma will totally want you involved in it no matter if you win or not. Then we can get Igor in on it too . . ."

"Wait, so you're saying I shouldn't win and I should let you win?" she said.

"No. I mean, yes . . . I mean . . . maybe," I said.

"You said, WWMMD, right? So what do you think my grandma would do?" she said.

"She would press the button!" I said.

Just as both of us were reaching for the button, Fang leaped out of my pocket and pounced on the button herself.

"Lava sequence initiated." A computerized voice

came out from a speaker above the box. Fang's fur stood on end as she sat on the red button still hidden from the others' view by the sides of the box.

The room went eerily quiet. Everyone stopped fighting and stared up at the two of us standing on the table with the box on it.

"That's not what I expected to happen," I said.

13

Immediately, a circular plastic shield started to slide up around the table, sealing Geeky Girl and me off from the rest of the group. Boris took off Geeky Girl's shoulder and pecked the plastic but there was nothing he could do.

He landed back on Geeky Girl's shoulder as everyone started pounding on the shield.

"Lava sequence initiated," the voice said again.

"What did you do!" Bob shouted through the glass.

Geeky Girl and I looked

at each other, then down at a rigid Fang still frozen on the spot, then back up at each other.

"She did it!" "He did it!" we both shouted at the same time.

Ezmirelda looked over the side. "There is lava filling up the volcano crater, people. Actual lava."

"We have to get out of here," Sanj said.

"Urgh, urgh," Igor said.

I tried to break the plastic sealing us in. Boris pecked with his beak. I lifted Fang out of the box and held her up to the side of the plastic tube that was facing away from the others so they couldn't see her.

"Come on, Fang, your claws must be able to cut through this," I said. Fang clawed at it with her super sharp claws, but it hardly scratched. "Wow, this Impenetrable Plastic 'R' Us stuff is really impenetrable," I said, dropping Fang into my pocket again.

Igor even tried to smash the plastic with all his strength, but it wouldn't budge.

"You guys try to escape. We'll figure

something out!" I shouted. "Right?" I turned to Geeky Girl.

She was still staring at the button.

Then I heard a snapping and a scratching of claws in the floor. And they weren't kitten claws.

"The dragon is awake," Diablo shouted.

"So, we are trapped in a room with rising lava and a dragon. Thanks, guys. Really, thanks," Bob said.

"The singing worked before. Just keep singing to him, and he'll go back to sleep," I shouted through the glass.

I could hear strains of "Twinkle, Twinkle, Evil Star" in harmony coming through the wall. It didn't sound bad. I yawned.

I could hear Ezmirelda saying, "Aw, he is a cute evil dragon when he's sleeping, isn't he?"

"So, what happens now?" I said to Geeky Girl.

Then a large package zoomed down the tube toward Geeky Girl and me. It stopped just above our heads and unwrapped itself.

"Congratulations," said a voice that sounded

like a recording of Madame Mako. "You have made the choice and pressed the button. Now you and only you have the ability to rise triumphantly out of the crater whereas the others must descend. 'Some are born ruthless, some achieve ruthlessness and some have ruthlessness thrust upon them.' That has now happened to you. Embrace the ruthlessness and use these wings to fly out of the crater and off to start your new life as my evil successor. Happy flying."

The package contained a pair of jet wings that would carry one person. One person could fly away. Geeky Girl or me. That's why only one person could push the button.

"But what about the others?" I said.

"The voice said that they have to descend. That's how they escape. They have to go down to get out from the lava," Geeky Girl said.

"But that doesn't make sense. The lava is coming up," I said.

"Maybe you could fly off and get help. And take Fang?"

"I wouldn't be able to get help in time," she said. "We have to figure out how to get everyone out of here. How can we get them up to the surface?"

"Well, there is lava rising fast and there are no ladders up from here or out there," I said.

"That's it—ladders. Chutes and ladders. There are no ladders but there are chutes," she said.

"The chutes that take you down into the volcano? But that's down into the lava," I said.

"They are the tubular slides that go down to that floor with the room with the Lose/Exit sign. They are the way out if you lose. We just have to make everybody lose," she said.

"The only problem is that they are still heading into the lava. That's not good," she added.

"It's OK. The slides are made out of the same impenetrable stuff that this plastic shield is. They have the same sticker on them. I saw it," I said. "It should be safe. They can slide down and get out."

Geeky Girl nodded.

"OK, guys," I shouted through the plastic wall. "We have a plan. So, you kinda have to make the slides appear and then go down into the lava."

"That is a terrible plan," Sanj said.

"The worst plan ever," Ezmirelda added.

"Urgh, urgh, urgh," Igor said.

"OK, I know it doesn't make sense, Igor, but there is no way to get up, so the only way to escape is to go down. The slides are completely encased in that impenetrable plastic, so they should take you down to the very bottom basement of the volcano where Geeky Girl and I saw an exit."

"OK, so even if we did believe your go-down-into-the-lava plan. How do we make the slides open up so we can use them?" Ezmirelda said.

"The rhyme," Geeky Girl shouted. "The rhyme said one false move and you fall through the floor. You and Dustin have to dance well to get the doors to open. Then go outside the door and everybody has to dance badly so the slides are activated."

Dustin looked over the side toward the rising lava. "We either try their plan or just wait to be consumed by the lava."

"Urgh, urgh, urgh, urgh, urgh?" Igor asked.

"No, the room isn't made of the same impenetrable plastic as this tube around us or the slides. It doesn't have the same sticker. I don't think the room you're in is gonna be lavaproof. You guys have to try," I said.

"Urgh, urgh, urgh?" Igor added.

"What about us?" I said. "Ummm . . . we're still figuring that one out. We'll see you back at camp. Now go."

Dustin and Ezmirelda started the dance and

the doors opened just as before. Once out on the
landing, they all got ready to dance badly.

"I don't know if I can dance badly," Dustin
said.

"I could stomp on your feet and then you
would have to dance badly," Ezmirelda said.

"I think I'll try." Dustin gulped.

Then Ezmirelda spotted Lucky still curled up
on the floor. "Hey, what about the dragon?" she
said.

"The dragon is sound asleep. He won't try and follow us. We'll be safe," Bob said.

"No, I mean we're not leaving him here to become a dragon-lava fritter. He's coming." Ezmirelda tried to lift the sleeping dragon, but he wouldn't budge.

Igor shrugged and walked over to Lucky, gently hoisted him into a fireman's carry over his shoulder and started to stomp.

We watched as one by one Dustin, Sanj, Bob, Diablo and Ezmirelda danced really, really terribly. Like the worst dad-dancing at a wedding that you could imagine. And one by one they all fell through the floor and down one of the impenetrable plastic slides. The last one to fall was Igor. He gave us a nod and gripped Lucky in a strong bear hug as the floor dropped away and he was gone.

"OK, so that either worked or we just sent all of our friends and our enemies crashing down into a bath of fire," Geeky Girl said.

"Hey, I think Bath of Fire is one of the metal bands that Bob plays sometimes," I said.

"Reeeeooooowwwwlll!" Fang jumped against the plastic wall and scratched as hard as she could.

"It won't work, kitten. We can't break it." I looked at Geeky Girl. "There is only one way out of here for us, and that's up. With the wings."

"But it will only take one of us," she said.

"Maybe." I paused. "So what have we learned so far from this game of your grandmother's?" I asked.

"That Grandma has a thing for board games and overly dramatic bad rhymes?" Geeky Girl said.

"Yeah, definitely that. But also, that if you think you aren't gonna win, what would any self-respecting evil scientist do to change that?" I asked.

"Cheat!" we said together.

"So let's see what I've got left in my backpack of inventions that might help." I sat down on the tabletop and started to unpack while Geeky Girl got the jet wings ready to use.

I had one nearly used-up spray can of Insta-Sticky.

One Invisible Lair Trap Detector.

A bunch of Grandma's peanut butter cookies.

And a piece of string.

Geeky Girl looked at the stuff all spread out on the table.

"OK, we don't have enough of the sticky stuff to use to climb out, right?" she said.

"Right," I said.

"Maybe I can reconfigure the Invisible Lair Trap Detector to help us?" Geeky Girl said.

"We are already in a trap," I said. "I figured that out without the detector."

"Then we have to use the jet pack," Geeky Girl said.

"But that will only take one of us," I said.

"If we use it as a jet pack," she agreed. "But what if we use it to start an explosion?"

"Um, then we would die in the explosion instead of dying by lava," I said.

"Meoooow," Fang agreed.

"No, we slide the jet pack under the table and puncture it at the same time as we start a spark. It will ignite and blast us up out of the tube," she said.

"Or it will ignite and blast us to kingdom come," I said.

Geeky Girl gave me a look.

"It's a thing my grandma says, OK? It means we'll blow up," I added. I reached down to console myself from our impending death with a peanut butter cookie. That's when I saw the sticker.

"Hang on, the table is made of the same impenetrable plastic." I pointed to the sticker. "If we are all on this side of the table when the blast goes off underneath, then we should be protected," I said.

"And it should be enough force to blast us out of the volcano," she said.

"And Fang and Boris?" I asked.

"You can put Fang in one pocket and Boris in the other. They can grip on with their claws so they don't fall out," she said. "I think it's our only shot."

"OK, we can stick the jet pack canisters under the table with the last bit of Insta-Sticky spray," I said.

We could feel the heat of the lava through the plastic walls of the tube. "OK, let's do it," I said.

We took the wings off the jet pack and rigged the canisters to propel us up out of the tube. We slid them down the sides of the table and we secured them under the table with the sticky stuff. It was a tight squeeze to get it down there, and neither of us could fit under the table to set off the explosion.

"Lava incursion imminent," the voice said.

"We know," Geeky Girl said.

"Breach of wall in one minute," it said.

"We got it!" I shouted at the voice.

I reached my arm down under the table but couldn't get near enough and definitely couldn't puncture the tanks. Fang jumped down next to the jet pack canister. She sharpened her claws on the floor.

"Fang, do you think you can puncture the jet pack?" I asked.

"Reeeeooooowwwll," she purred.

"But we need a spark to ignite it," Geeky Girl said. "Do you have any matches?"

"No," I said. "Must remember to add matches to my bag of evil gadgets."

"You bring peanut butter cookies but not matches?" she said.

While we were arguing Boris flapped down onto the table. He chipped his beak against the metal clasp on my backpack and it made a spark.

"Pretty cool," I said.

"Yeah, but too dangerous. If Boris creates the spark down under the table, he'll go up in the explosion," she said.

"What if we had a fuse that Boris could light while he's up here safely out of the way?" I said, and held up the string.

"Lava breach in thirty seconds," the voice said.

"OK, let's try," Geeky Girl said.

I passed the end of the string down to Fang, who laid it next to the canister. Fang bared her claws and got ready to puncture the tank. Boris had his beak over the clasp.

"Ready?!" Geeky Girl shouted.

"Lava breach in ten seconds," the voice said.

"Go!" I said.

Boris nodded to Fang, and she clawed. Her razor-sharp claw went straight through the coating on the tank. Gas seeped out.

Fang nodded and jumped up onto the table, out of the way of the spark.

Boris chipped the metal clasp, and a spark flew into the air and caught the end of the string, and the spark sped down the fuse under the table.

The pets jumped into my pockets. We heard the voice say, "Three, two . . ." and then we were off!

15

It was like riding a surfboard on top of a hurricane. Geeky Girl held on to the wings she had taken off the jet pack, and I had my backpack on with the Trap Detector in my hand.

As we neared the top of the crater, we could see the lava rising up next to us.

"Here we go!" I shouted as the explosion propelled us up and out of the volcano top!

We were flying!

You know the expression "What goes up, must come down"?

Well, we had gone up, so there was only one thing left.

We were free from the lava crater, but our new problem was that we were now falling toward the outside of the volcano. Geeky Girl extended the wings to slow our descent. It was working. We were heading toward a sandy slope.

I patted Fang on the head as she peeked out of my pocket. "Hold on, little one," I said. "It's gonna get even bumpier."

"Have you ever sand-boarded?" I shouted to Geeky Girl.

"No!" she yelled.

"Well, get ready to learn! Lean when I lean and close the wings when we touch down. Ready? Here we go."

Geeky Girl let the wings drop as we touched down on the sand, and we started to slide. The table legs were burned off in the explosion (guess they weren't made of the plastic stuff), so when the tabletop hit the ground, it acted like a surfboard.

"Wooooo!" I shouted as we sped down the hill.

"Head for the water!" Geeky Girl shouted from behind me on the tabletop. "We can slide right into the lake and it will break our fall."

Then suddenly the Trap Detector started pinging. "Oh great. It's detecting traps on the slope of the volcano!" I shouted.

"Lean left!" I yelled as we banked sideways to avoid some spikes that popped up in front of us.

"Go right!" I said as a trapdoor opened up in our path.

"More security traps?" I shouted.

"She probably wasn't thinking there would be people breaking out of her volcano lair," she answered.

We were now nearly at the lake. "OK, Boris, you might want to fly off before we hit the water," I said. "And, Fang, you don't like swimming too much either, do you? Why don't you hitch a ride?" Boris gripped the scruff of Fang's neck and they fluttered off.

"I'll put up the wings again to slow us before we hit the water," Geeky Girl yelled.

We slowed a little and then—sppplooooosh!—we were in the lake.

I must have blacked out for a second, because the next thing I remembered someone threw me a life preserver labeled "Evil Aqua Rescue." I grabbed it and let myself be towed to the side of the lake. Trevor hoisted me out of the water. "Zat vas not vhat ve expected," he said. "Vhen Madame Mako brought us out here to vitness ze victor fly out to claim zher prize, we did not expect two of you. Nor did ve expect to have to rescue ze vinners."

Then I looked over and Kirsty was pulling Geeky Girl out of the lake a few yards down. Her grass skirt was singed from the heat of the explosion and she was soaking wet, but she was smiling.

"We did it," she said. "We won."

I walked over to her "Yeah, that was not really how I saw us winning. You know, less lava and near death and water would have been better."

"Agreed," she said. "But we did it."

Madame Mako then stepped out onto the shore, holding a remote control in her hand. She pressed a button and the bridge extended as before.

She walked up to Geeky Girl and smiled. "You have earned the right to be my successor," she said. "Maybe you did it in a slightly unconventional way and you weren't as completely ruthless as I would have liked, but we can work on that." She looked over at me. "But you did it, and I suppose this means that as you both completed the test, you both get to become my successors and take over my empire." Her face had gone back to the slightly irritated face rather than the smiling one.

It didn't matter, though. She said that Geeky Girl and I had won. We had beaten the odds and both of us had made it through. We would be epic at running an empire.

We could both have crowns and everyone could still call me Emperor Mark. We had gone from going out the Lose door to flying out the top of the volcano.

Then it hit me. The Lose door.

16

"What about the others?" I said.

"Have you seen them?" Geeky Girl asked.

Madame Mako nodded. "I saw on the sensors that they landed safely in the volcano base earlier. I didn't check how many were there, though, and I didn't open the door to let them out, because it would ruin the suspense. I wanted to see who would fly out the top. I had not anticipated two flying out, though. They might as well come out now."

Trevor walked over to the side of the volcano, looking for an emergency exit sign.

"Here, let me." Kirsty karate-kicked the door, and the vibrations crumbled the rock around it.

We rushed over. We could hear voices inside.

"Apparently someone is trying to break in just when we are trying to break out," Dustin said.

"Urgh, urgh, urgh!" Igor shouted.

"He said, 'Stand back,'" I echoed as Igor kicked the door from his side just as Madame Mako pressed another button on her remote control. The door burst open.

Igor, Bob, Diablo, Dustin, Sanj and Ezmirelda all walked out onto the shore.

"Igor, you are stronger that I thought!" Sanj said.

Igor smiled.

Madame Mako walked over. "No, he is not. I did that."

Igor slumped his massive shoulders. "Urgh."

She continued. "You have all lost the contest. You may go back to your camp now," she said. "It was a pleasure testing you."

"Testing, we don't mind, but it was no pleasure being trapped in a volcano that's filling with lava," Ezmirelda said.

"The slides are impenetrable. The lava was just there for effect. You can't have a volcano lair without a lava trap." She shook her head.

"Anyway, we took Lucky with us too," Ezmirelda said.

"I would have whistled for him and he would have gone down a slide too." Madame Mako shook her head. "None of you were ruthless enough."

"I just want to say that I was completely against taking the lizard, but she insisted," Sanj said.

Lucky strode up next to Ezmirelda and licked her hand. She reached down and scratched him under the chin.

"Hmmmm . . . you are all here and you have all your limbs. So he didn't even bite anyone?" she said, shaking her head. "I suppose Lucky is not as fierce as I had thought."

Ezmirelda stepped forward. "Lucky is the fiercest pet Komodo ever, and I think he's decided that he needs an owner who appreciates him. Don't you, boy?"

Madame Mako got out her whistle. "Heel, Lucky," she said, and blew.

He rolled over on the beach and Ezmirelda stroked his tummy.

"I think he made up his mind," I added.

Phillipe spoke, "But you can't take on an evil pet Komodo dragon. They are not allowed at camp."

Lucky stood and walked toward Phillipe, backing him up against a palm tree. He reared and stood with his claws on Phillipe's chest and breathed dragon breath in his face. "Unless . . . perhaps the dragon could be employed by the camp as a guard dragon? Maybe?" Phillipe said.

Fang slunk over from the bushes and jumped back into my pocket. She looked over at Lucky standing up to Phillipe and made a little purr. I think that was a bit of mutual evil-pet respect going on there.

Kirsty and Trevor walked up to Phillipe. Lucky turned to them and hissed. Kirsty tried to land a kick to knock him off Phillipe, but Lucky thwacked her with his tail and she hit the ground with a thud.

Kirsty smiled as she got up and dusted off the sand. "He would make a good guard."

"Well, maybe he doesn't want to stay," Ezmirelda said. "Maybe I want to go home and teach my new evil dragon some wicked evil tricks." Lucky hissed one more time at Phillipe, then pulled back and walked over to her side, and Phillipe started to breathe again. "We'll think about it," she said, and patted Lucky on the head.

Madame Mako turned to me and Geeky Girl again.

"This entire exercise is most irregular. You weren't at all ruthless in there. You helped each other? I don't understand," she said.

"I know," Geeky Girl said. "But we can work on that.

"Grandma, you said friends are a hindrance, but I don't agree. They are the ones who have your back when you need it most."

Madame Mako shook her head.

Geeky Girl smiled. "Grandma, I don't think I want to run your evil empire or any evil empire. I don't ever want to be as ruthless as you've had to be to do this."

Madame Mako looked kinda hurt and disappointed. "Glenda, if you give up the empire, then you will be stopping your henchman from winning it as well. Is that what you want?" she said, and turned to me.

"Mark," I said, "the name is Mark. I personally think I would be epic at ruling an evil empire and flying a volcanic island lair," I said. "And I think Geeky Girl would be epic at it too."

17

"But for some mad, un-evil reason, that's not what she wants to do, so I guess I have to live with that," I said. "And it's not like this is going to be my only chance to rule an evil empire. That will happen again." I smiled. "But ya know, if you had a spare crown lying around, I could take that off your hands."

Then I spotted a bit of the metal wing twisted into a crescent on the ground that must have broken off in the crash. "Or maybe I don't have to wait for someone else to give me a crown," I said, and picked it up, blew the sand off it and put it on. Well, it would have to do for now, anyway.

Igor smiled. "Urgh, urgh, urgh," he said.

"Yeah, I knew it would suit me. Thanks." I nodded.

Madame Mako looked puzzled. "I don't understand young people nowadays. In my day, you would not look an evil gift horse in the mouth like this." She shook her head.

I leaned in and whispered to her, "And you know, it's not all bad. You didn't find a successor, but you did find your granddaughter." I paused. "Who I know is standing right here, so she isn't exactly lost, but I was making a point . . ."

"You need to know when to stop talking, henchman, I mean Mark," she said, and gave me a very, very, very slight smile. But ya know, I'll take that.

"Then who will take over the volcano island?" Bob said, totally killing the moment.

"I would do a fantastic job running the island," Sanj said. "And I could pick up the evil elephant research where you left off, Madame Mako."

"I would be the best to run this island. Can you imagine a wresting ring in the center of the volcano!" Diablo added.

"Obviously, I would be best," Dustin said. "Just because I'm me."

Madame Mako turned to walk away from all the campers telling her how fantastic they would be. Her mildly irritated face was tipping into pretty fed up. As she turned and headed for the bridge off the island, she dropped her remote control.

"Madame Mako! Wait!" Sanj rushed forward, picked up the remote and was just about to hand it to her as she stepped onto the bridge when he stopped.

"I just need to show you how well I could control this island if it were my empire," he said. "With this much power, I could do amazing things. You'll see."

Sanj started pressing buttons on the remote. The volcano started to shake, and then boulders started shooting out from the crater and raining down on the shore.

"Run for cover!" Trevor shouted.

Trevor and the counselors herded everyone under an outcropping of rock so they were a bit protected, but that meant they couldn't see us or Sanj standing on the shoreline jumping up and down and hitting random buttons.

"Oh no. That's not it. Let me try this button," Sanj said, pushing more.

The bridge that Madame Mako was standing on suddenly retracted back into the island, dropping her into the water. She flapped about in the lake, trying to avoid the falling boulders.

Geeky Girl immediately jumped into the water after her grandma.

She swam out to her, but the two of them couldn't get back to shore with the boulders landing on the island, and Madame Mako was looking tired. Geeky Girl couldn't drag her back on her own.

Then I spotted the life preserver that Trevor had used to pull me out.

"Hang on!" I shouted. I threw the life preserver, attached to a rope, out to Geeky Girl and she grabbed hold. She got Madame Mako to hold on to it too, and I started pulling them toward the shore. But the boulders kept flying and Geeky Girl kept having to stop to avoid rocks crashing into the lake.

"We need cover!" I shouted.

The next thing I knew, Igor was running into the water with the Canoe of Shame hoisted above his head. He held it over Geeky Girl and Madame Mako like a shield as I started pulling them in.

None of us were safe until Sanj stopped firing boulders out of the volcano, though. This could not get any worse.

Then of course as soon as I thought that.

It got worse.

"Maybe it's this button!" Sanj shouted as he pressed another spot on the remote.

The volcano island suddenly started to shake. It sounded like engines were revving up. It was getting ready to take off! With us standing near the edge and Igor, Geeky Girl and Madame Mako still in the water.

"Fang!" I shouted. "You need to get that remote off Sanj!"

Fang let out a "Reeeoowwlll" like a battle cry, and she and Boris headed for Sanj.

Boris flew around his head, batting him with his wings. "Get off me, you ridiculous sky rat!" Sanj shouted. While he was distracted, Fang pounced and grabbed the remote in her mouth.

18

Fang ran back to me and dropped the remote control at my feet.

There were loads of buttons, but one that clearly said "Boulders."

"Seriously, Sanj?" I shouted. "You couldn't have figured that one out?"

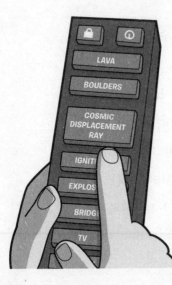

There were loads of other buttons, though. "Ignition." "Explosion." "Cosmic Displacement Ray."

Oh man, that sounded way too cool. It was all I could do to stop myself from pressing "Cosmic Displacement Ray" just to see what it would do.

I pressed the "Ignition" button because I figured that was probably the button that started the engines, so maybe the same button would switch them off. If I was designing an evil volcano island remote control, then that's the way I would work it. Of course, I would also put an Anti-Sanj Theft Device on it so it would leap out of his hands if he ever got hold of it. Simple evil precautions can prevent lots of hassle, you know.

Immediately, the engines powered down and the island stopped shaking. "Phew," I said, and then pressed the "Boulders" button too.

The boulders stopped and I was finally able to heave the rope to pull Madame Mako and Geeky Girl back on shore. Boris fluttered up to Geeky Girl and fanned her face with his wings. "I'm OK, Boris," she said.

"Now you and Fang get out of here before anyone else sees you."

Igor put down the canoe and helped Madame Mako back onto her feet while Boris and Fang headed back to the shrub. I could see two sets of little eyes looking at us through the leaves.

The others all came out from under the outcrop once the counselors confirmed that the boulders had definitely stopped. They ran up to Madame Mako.

Phillipe took her hand. "Are you all right, Madame Mako?" he asked.

"No thanks to you hiding the whole time," she said, pulling back her hand. "I owe my life to my granddaughter and her henchmen." She stopped. "I mean her friends." It looked like it physically hurt her to say the word. I felt her pain.

"Urgh, urgh," Igor said, and smiled.

"He said, 'No problem,'" I translated. "And same for me."

"Oh, and please thank your little feathered friend and the evil cat," Madame Mako said to Geeky Girl. "They helped too."

Trevor, Phillipe and Kirsty all turned to Madame Mako. "Did you spot a pet, besides the dragon, on the island, Madame Mako?" Kirsty asked.

"Ummm, I think Madame Mako means the wild bird and wild cat that must have arrived with the flying island," I said.

"Yes," Geeky Girl said, "it's the indigenous tropical bird and wild island cat. I saw them too." She nodded toward Madame Mako with her eyes saying, "This is the story, OK? Stick to it!"

Madame Mako sighed.

"They must have been spooked by all the boulders," Geeky Girl added.

"Their bird and cat attacked me! They have very illegal and very dangerous pets that go around attacking people with remote controls!" Sanj was screaming. "You have to believe me!"

"I didn't see any pets other than my very hungry Komodo dragon here." Ezmirelda strode over to Sanj. Lucky licked his shoes and drooled on them.

"But they took the remote right out of my hand. They attacked me," Sanj continued.

"I think you were in such a panic, you only thought you saw them attack you." She glared at him. "Of course, if Lucky here had taken the remote out of your hand, then you wouldn't still have a hand, would you? Am I making myself clear?" Ezmirelda leaned into Sanj, and Lucky scratched the ground slowly with his claw.

"I think Ezmirelda is correct." Sanj gulped. "I was in such a panic, I was seeing things." He backed away.

"So, you just saw some vild animals from ze island, Madame Mako?" Trevor asked.

"Yes, that must be it." Madame Mako nodded and smiled at Geeky Girl.

Then she turned to Ezmirelda. "I'm happy that you are looking after Lucky. I think you will be a strong influence on him." She looked down at Lucky. "Farewell." She turned back to Ezmirelda, handing her a card. "Oh, and here's the number of his manicurist. You'd be surprised how hard it is to get a decent manicure for a dragon these days."

Kirsty walked over to Ezmirelda. "So what did you decide? Are you staying at camp with the dragon as an official guard dragon?" She reached down like she was going to try to pet Lucky, but his growling changed her mind. "Or do we send you both back home in the Canoe of Shame?"

"Let me think." Ezmirelda looked at the canoe and then down at Lucky. Lucky scratched his claw along the dirt and then rolled over on his back like he wanted a tummy rub.

"Some guard dragon," Dustin mumbled.

In a second, Lucky was on his feet and over to Dustin. He hissed a low hiss that grew in volume as he got closer step-by-step to a now-quaking Dustin.

"Or maybe he is? Maybe he's a really good guard dragon? Who's a good guard dragon?!" Dustin shouted. "Please get him off me."

"I think Lucky would be an epic guard dragon," I said to Ezmirelda.

"Yeah, I would feel safe knowing he was around," Geeky Girl added. "I mean not 'in my

tent' around, but, you know, 'at the entrance of the
camp' around." She smiled at Ezmirelda.

"Urgh, urgh, urgh," said Igor.

"Yeah, good call, Igor," I said. "Camp

Mwhaaa-haa-ha-a-watha would get some serious respect from any other camps if we had our own dragon. Serious respect."

"There are actually other evil scientist camps?" Geeky Girl asked. "Never mind. I just wanted to say that if the camp needs Lucky, then Lucky needs you. So maybe you should stay. If you want?"

"Do I really want to compete with a bunch of squabbling kids for a camp crown?" Ezmirelda said.

"Why does everyone keep dissing the crown?! It's a crown, people," I said.

"Maybe I should stay, though. You know, to make sure Lucky is happy as a guard dragon," she added.

"I think zee dragon vill let us know if he iz not happy," Trevor said.

"OK, great. Could somebody get him away from me now," Dustin cried.

"Lucky, heel." Ezmirelda patted her leg. Lucky trotted over but was scrabbling in the dirt for something.

Madame Mako spoke. "He is hungry. He didn't

get to eat that boy like he thought." She pointed to Dustin, and Dustin sunk to the floor.

"I have something," I said, and pulled out the last few peanut butter cookies from my backpack. I threw one to Lucky, and he caught it midair.

"Who's a clever dragon," Ezmirelda gushed as she rubbed his chin.

I gave her the rest of the cookies. "He looks like he might want more," I said.

While everyone was distracted watching Lucky jump for cookies, I snuck over to the bush and let Fang jump into my coat pocket.

"You better get back to camp while you can too," I said to Boris, and he fluttered off toward the tents on the other side of the bridge.

Then I walked over and handed Madame Mako the remote and she pushed the bridge button to reactivate the land bridge back to camp.

Madame Mako spoke to the counselors, "I think my time here is complete. Watch out for that lot," she said pointing to all of us. "There are a few bright evil sparks in the bunch."

19

"Zank you, Madame Mako," Trevor said, and they all bowed and went to the other side of the bridge, leaving just the campers on the island. Igor, Geeky Girl and I walked to the edge of the bridge with Madame Mako as the others started to cross.

"Thank you, Glenda," Madame Mako said. "I don't understand you, but I would like to get to know you more perhaps."

"I would like that too," Geeky Girl said. "But I still think you should look into retiring, Grandma."

"You could come with me and stay on the island." She looked around at all the smashed boulders. "When it's fixed up, of course."

"I don't want to move to a flying volcano island, but I might like to come and visit," she said. "But I think you need company. Maybe it would be good to be with some friends," Geeky Girl said.

Madame Mako shuddered. "Don't push it . . . Evil colleagues, perhaps," she said.

"I've sometimes thought that the island might make a very good retirement home for evil scientists. There must be other evil scientists in my position of wanting to downsize their evil empires

as they reach a certain age. A flying volcano island might have appeal. And it would certainly help with the bills. This place is not cheap to run," she said.

"So, nobody wins?" Bob asked.

"Nobody gets the evil empire?" Sanj asked.

"Or the volcano island?" Diablo asked. "Maybe the old evil guys would like a wrestling ring in the crater. I still think it's a good idea."

"I'll think about it," Madame Mako said. "The

doctors said I should exercise. Maybe a bit of combat will keep me active. Right, I best get the island off to the flying volcano island garage and get it fixed up."

Madame Mako held out her arms. "Now give your grandma a nice, big evil—" She stopped herself. "Well, a hug, anyway."

Geeky Girl hugged her and the rest of us bowed.

We headed over the bridge and she pressed the button to retract it. She waved as she stepped back through the front door and fired up the engines for takeoff.

The ground shuddered and quaked as the island heaved itself out of the lake and back up into the sky. The shadow of the island fell over the camp, and I could feel Fang in my pocket start to tense up, but then relax. I think the kitten was worn out from our epic evil night on the island.

The noise of the takeoff must have woken the rest of the camp, because soon everyone was out

of their tents, looking up at the sky as the island
rose higher and higher.

The sun was coming up over the lake as the island flew off into the distance.

As we were walking back to our tents, Bob shouted out to Trevor ahead of us, "So who won then? Who got Evil Emperor of the Week?"

"I think I deserve it because I had the best plans," Sanj said.

"Urgh, urgh, urgh, urgh, urgh, urgh," Igor said.

"Yeah, but you nearly crushed us all with falling boulders," I translated.

"It doesn't matter. Ze people Madame Mako declared ze vinners would be disqualified for completely un-evil behavior so ze challenge vas never actually completed, really. Zere can be no vinner," Trevor said.

Phillipe came running back from the mess tent toward our group as the other campers started to gather around. "Good news!" he said. "As you can see, unfortunately, Madame Mako had to pull out as our guest celebrity villain at the last minute, but we have secured a replacement."

Kirsty stood next to Phillipe. "Tim the

Terrifying will be joining us this afternoon."

Phillipe continued, "He was just sitting around, waiting for his evil phone to ring apparently. In the meantime, we have a video in the mess tent on the importance of accurate evil plan management."

Most people's faces looked a bit like Madame Mako's not-very-impressed face. "This isn't a request, people. You HAVE to go. Move it!" Kirsty shouted.

The campers groaned and headed toward the mess tent.

When everyone but us had gone into the mess tent, Boris fluttered over to Geeky Girl and landed on her shoulder.

"They are gonna feed us while we watch the video, right?" I asked. "I'm hungrier than a Komodo dragon right now." Fang poked her head out of my pocket and meowed. "And Fang is too."

Geeky Girl was staring up into the air, watching the island fade from view.

"Urgh, urgh, urgh?" Igor asked.

"He said, 'Do you think you'll see your grandma again soon?'" I said.

"I think so," she said. "She might try to make me more like her and I might try to make her more like me. I think we could both learn a lot from each other, though," she said.

"You are still soooooo lucky to have a famous evil grandma like that," I said. "I mean, you'll be dropping by the volcano island after school for a sandwich and a bit of boulder shooting. How cool is that?"

"I think it's just nice to have a grandmother. Whatever kind of grandmother she is. I've never had that really before," she said.

"I love my grandma and all, but a grandma in a condo in the suburbs versus a grandma in a flying volcano island evil lair . . ."

"Or Flying Volcano Island Evil Retirement Community?" Geeky Girl corrected.

"Yeah, whichever. It's still cool," I said. "Now, let's get some food."

"Urgh, urgh," Igor said.

"I am epically hungry too," I said.

"Heh, do you think we should try the brain-jelly-tick thing on Tim the Terrifying when he gets here, Igor?" I said as we headed into the tent.

"Urghy, urghy, urghy," Igor agreed.

Dear Grandma,

I'm having lots of fun at summer camp.

    We went on a trip that made me think of you.

    Thought that maybe you could send some more of those cookies you make with the squishy peanut butter middle. oh, and some crown polish.

    Thanks,

                              Mark

P.S. Have you ever considered selling the condo and renting an apartment in a used flying volcano island? Just an idea.

Mark is doing okay against Evil Scientist Summer Camp,
but annoying little brothers are a different story . . .

For more FIN-TASTICALLY FISHY mayhem, check out: